Rockhaven
SUMMER

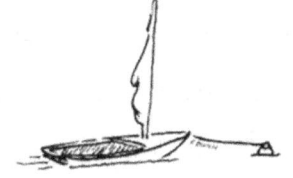

Farley Dunn

THREE SKILLET

ROCKHAVEN SUMMER, Dunn, Farley L

First Edition

A Katie Carver Novel

 THREE SKILLET

www.ThreeSkilletPublishing.com

v.5

ISBN 978-1-943189-03-8

Enjoy all the Katie Carver novels:

Rockhaven Summer

Rockhaven Wedding

Rockhaven Christmas

Rockhaven Spring

Author's Note

Those of you familiar with Mid-Coast Maine will recognize elements of Vinalhaven Island in my Rockhaven series, but only because of my family history and the summers I've spent there. If you do visit Vinalhaven someday, look for Rockhaven. You'll find that magical place strewn all about the craggy shoreline and in the stalwart people that call Vinalhaven home.

1

Katie Carver's hair blew across her face, and she pulled it away with slender, delicate fingers. The thick strands were long and dark, and they glistened when they caught in the wind.

They also caught on her broken nails.

When one brushed against her cheek, she tore her eyes from the familiar scenery rushing by at breakneck speed and glanced at it. The polish, gleaming Brandywine with an iridescent sheen, was so inappropriate for today's trip, as proven by the damage she'd already inflicted on them. It was proof, in a way, that she was still the island girl she'd tried so hard to leave behind. She was still Katherine Daytona Carver, of the Rockhaven Carvers, one of the moneyed set who no longer had money, just the name that everyone still knew.

"Katie? Or do you go by Katherine, now? Or maybe it's Dame Carver, newest owner of Carver Point?"

The words laughed at her; she could hear it, and she fought the tears. She would not let Jeffrey Ragsdale know he could still manipulate her like a child's toy, even after all these years. He had been Jeff to his island friends, but she had never dared more than his full name. He had only been a year older, but it had been a gap she'd never bridged, with him always staying just out of reach, whether at seven, eleven, or fourteen. He was the wild island boy who knew every submerged rock ledge, every dripping spruce, and just where to find the thickest stands of island roses.

She had idolized him as a child, worshipped him as a preteen, and thought she'd loved him at fourteen. Then her world had been stolen from her. The call. Her grandmother's house burned to its foundations, and the Boston funeral attended by Boston society. The whole time she'd wanted to return to the Point to cry her desperate tears, but at fourteen, well, who listens to anyone at fourteen?

She hadn't been back. Her parents had blamed the island and its narrow roads for Grandmother Carver's death. Katie knew differently. She had been the cause. She hadn't been there, and for that reason, her world had been stolen from her.

Now Jeffrey made fun of her. *Jeff.* Jeff made fun of her. She would call him Jeff. At the town float, he'd held his tanned hand out to her as she stepped on his boat, and he'd said, "Jeff, if you please. Never Jeffrey. That's a boy's name." He'd grinned as he said it, though, as if he were teasing a little pigtailed girl.

8

"Call me Dame Carver again, Jeff Ragsdale, and I'll push you over the side." She bit the final word off, but she would. It was hard enough being on this boat with the boy she'd once thought she'd loved. To have him make fun of her at the same time? It was intolerable.

"I remember a little girl who cried when she picked the roses up at Sommer's Ledge."

"She did not." But even as she said the words, she realized she was rubbing at the side of one finger that still carried a scar. One of the thorns had gotten infected, and the town doctor had lanced it in the middle of the night. She'd never told any of her friends for fear of their ridicule.

"Did, too." The laughter was still there. "I picked out a few thorns, and I'm certain I remember a tear or two. Could have been appreciation running down those cheeks, though. Yeah, I bet that was it. Appreciation for the island boy willing to take the time for a little bloody finger."

He was silent for a time. They were crossing the ferry's wake, and as they rode up one side of the swell, things in the boat shifted. Katie grabbed for her weekend case, only to have the nose of the boat fall just as she leaned over, crashing into the sea and sending a wall of spray over the bow of the boat. Water dripped off the wheelhouse onto her jeans, darkening the fabric in expanding concentric circles. The engine revved, and the boat skewed sideways before biting into the sea again and smoothing out.

"That was a blast!" Jeff laughed. "Want to do it

again?" He pointed to the far side of the wake, and he whipped the wheel sideways and gunned the engine.

"Stop it, Jeffrey!" Katie looked away. He was still doing it, reaching inside to manipulate feelings she had boxed up and put away over a decade ago. She had given them to God, and now . . . now they were rearing up again.

It seemed she didn't have a choice in the matter, though, because just then the boat hit the other side of the wake, only this time they didn't hit it dead on. The boat twisted sideways, violently, and Katie didn't have time to grab at anything to steady herself.

"Jeffrey!" The word was out of her mouth as she flew across the boat, hitting her shoulder on *something* before her foot slipped from under her and she col-lapsed—God forbid!—right against him. He laughed as he killed the throttle and reached to lift her up.

"Whoa! So, Jeffrey is here to stay, is he? I remem-ber a pretty little girl who used to follow me every-where who once called me that. I was fifteen. I don't think I'm fifteen anymore, but I haven't forgotten."

"I'm so sorry, *Jeff.*" She emphasized his name, and she laughed to show the incident was no big deal, as she stood and stepped away from him. "A lifetime ago I wouldn't have noticed that little wave. I guess I've lost my sea legs."

"You think?" His eyes watched her carefully. "No damage? Leg? Shoulder? Ego?" He grinned, though.

"The cabin?" She meant the one habitable structure left on her newly inherited property. Her question was a diversion. She needed to get off talking about the two of them. It didn't seem fourteen years were so far gone that she had severed all her emotional ties with that long-ago life. The truth of the matter? That life was another girl's life.

She felt the old bitterness rise, the one that wanted to blame it all on God. She had given it to Him, but only after months of tears and raging prayers blaming Him for not being there when He should have been. The bitterness had been harder to let go.

"So, the ego is damaged." Jeff was back at the wheel, and the thrub, thrub of the engine started up again. "Not *too* damaged, I hope. Not so damaged we can't plan a lobster bake this weekend."

He wasn't looking at her, but she could see the side of his face. As a boy, he'd been quick-footed and taut, with slabs for cheeks that crinkled into dimples when he smiled. Now? The dimples were deeper, and the sea had taken its toll. It had improved him, though, with laugh lines at the corners of his eyes, and windblown hair that whipped at his face but didn't quite block his vision. She glanced at his hand, the left one. Bare finger with no tan line. Well, at least they had something in common. She laughed sourly. Not by her choice, but there it was, anyway.

"I called Marc at the Paper Store. He said he'd send someone out." They were between Rockhaven and Settler's Island, and the water had flattened out. She watched the rocky shoreline speed past. Carver Point was at the north end of the island, and it was a good twenty-minute ride.

"He did."

"And?" She glanced at him. It was so easy to slip into the old patterns, with short answers that were mere suggestions of responses, leaving things half said and half understood at the same time.

"Just that." The laughter was in his words again.

"Okay. I'll find out when we get there." They passed the De Groot dock, a massive granite monstrosity that half the island envied and the rest decried as a blight on the shoreline. The house, an ancient shingled bear of a manse tucked into the trees, was visible just for a moment, then it slipped into the overgrowth and was gone. Even the dock with its undulating float soon disappeared into the rocky outcrops that broke up the shoreline. She had visited there with her grandmother on occasion, the gas lamps and cedar-paneled walls making it so very dark inside. She wondered for a minute who owned it now, if it had been sold or if it was still in the family.

Whatever, at least it was still there. She dreaded seeing the Point with its bare stone foundation. What memories would that bring? Running up the stone steps with Jennie hopping up after her? She smiled at that. She'd forgotten about her Flemish giant, as big as a small dog, cuddling in her bed at night. Who'd have thought a rabbit could reach upwards of fifty pounds? There were also all the things she had stored up from fourteen summers of memories, things she dreamed about every winter until she could get back to the island each year. Her grandmother had always been the lucky one, going out after the last snowfall, often in late March or early April and staying until the first real cold snap, sometimes in mid-November.

"At least I have the cabin." Katie let out a mournful sigh.

"You have what?" Jeff leaned over and called the words too loudly into her ear.

"The cabin." She placed her hand on his chest and pushed him away, and this time she smiled a real smile. "You heard me fine, and you keep your distance."

"Yes ma'am, Dame Carver."

She turned, ready to carry out her threat only to see a wide smile and deep dimples on his face. That had been on purpose. Well, she could give as well as she got.

"Just you wait, Jeff Ragsdale. You've got one coming." She pointed a broken fingernail at him.

"Yes, ma'am. This weekend will do fine by me. I'll even bring the lobster."

She laughed out loud at that one. "I'll bet you will." They were on his lobster boat, after all. That was the one thing he had more than enough of, lobster.

She contented herself for the rest of the journey to take in the shoreline. It was as familiar to her as her childhood, and it was as distant as a vengeful God could make it.

She had loved it once. She wouldn't let God take her memories, too, no matter how hard He tried.

She felt the tears rise again, and she tried to push the bitterness away. Why, God, she let herself think one harsh time. Then she allowed the beauty of her Maine island to fill her senses and force the pain away, at least for a while.

And Jeffrey. Why had he volunteered to bring her out? How odd was that? They hadn't seen each other in fourteen years. Well, she'd been firmly in control, she hadn't let her emotions slip, and once he dropped her off, with luck, she wouldn't need to see him again.

It was best that way, she told herself. Then, when she thought of him again, she told herself one more time, it would be better all around that she didn't see him again.

"This . . ." Katie stumbled over her words. "This. Who?" She felt her throat choke up. The dock . . . and the float. She had expected it to be . . . what, she didn't know, but not *repaired.*

"What, Dame Carver?" The laugh was still in the words.

"You know what I mean." Jeff's continual use of the term "dame" grated on her. "All this. No one's set foot on the Point for more than ten years. I expected this to be falling down."

Still, she was pleased. Boards had been replaced on the ramp, and the remembered lintel leading into the box at the top of the ramp still had the bell with its rope cord that had been there forever. At least she supposed it was the same. The wood looked fresh, though. All of it.

The crescent-shaped beach and the trees rearing up from the shoreline were the same. They were the very ones she and Jeff had clambered through over a decade of childhood, him always showing up with his friends the week she arrived, and like a pack of island wolves, prowling the shadowy nooks and crannies during the glorious months of summer.

The top of the hill was empty, though. Carver House should fill the skyline, a white canvas of porches and gables, with Grandpa Carver's rosebushes lining the foundation walls. All that was left was the sky and the wispy outline of clouds in the distance.

The boat glided up to the float, and the engines died away. She reached for a rope coiled on the float and looped it around a cleat on the boat. The movement felt as natural as if she'd left the island the previous summer and she was picking up where she'd left off.

"This one, too."

She turned, and Jeff held another line to her, this one to run from ship to shore. She reached for it, turning her head towards the float as she did, only to feel the warmth of another's fingers brush hers for a brief instant as the rope was dropped into her hand. She leaped onto the float and looped the line around a cleat in the old loop-loop-and-under fashion she'd learned as a girl, and at the same time glancing at the man who'd brought her out. He was turned away, his shirt tight across his back, as he pulled her few bags from the floor of the boat.

So, she thought. The touch, accidental, was just a

careless brush of finger to finger as a rope is passed from one hand to another. Nothing had been meant, and she would make nothing of it. Besides, there was nothing to make of it. If there had been anything to make of it, Jeff had missed his opportunity over a decade before.

She stood, aware of the sea smell, one of salt water and spruce, overlaid with wild roses and the sweetness of new-mown clover. That made her frown. New-mown clover. Then she saw it. The path up the hill, trimmed and green. Why was the path trimmed?

"Jeff?" She called to him, still searching with her eyes for anything else that didn't seem right. There. The old swing on the apple tree. It was still there, and it shouldn't be. Rope rots, and in fourteen years, it rots completely through. And the boathouse. There was still a boathouse right where it had always been. The doors were open, and it was empty, though.

"Yes, Dame?" The float rocked, and he stood at her side.

"I told you to stop that. Look at this." She swept the scene with an outstretched arm, stopping to point at the things, the odd things that weren't right. "What's wrong with this picture?"

"It's a pretty picture. I see nothing wrong with it. Why?"

She looked at him, her argument already rising in her throat, only to see his face right next to hers, watching her. His eyes, electric blue, and his laugh lines crinkled in a half smile. In that flash, she remembered the last time she'd seen him all those years ago.

August was playing its final tune, and in the heat of the afternoon, the gang had taken over the local swimming hole at the quarry. Jeff had been the wild boy of the bunch, in his cut-off jeans and bare shoulders, screaming like a cougar as he leaped from the rocks to thrash the water below.

She looked away, the intensity of how much she'd worshipped him then filling her with longing for something lost that could never be returned. The old anger at God gripped her, and she brushed her palm against her face to wipe an impending tear away.

"This. Someone's been out here." Her voice barely wavered, and for that she felt grateful.

"I should hope so." He chuckled. "It seems you did call Marc. Am I correct?"

What did that mean? Her call had only been to make sure the cabin was usable. Storms did happen on Rockhaven, and the cabin was right at the water's edge. Grandfathered at the water's edge. And if it were gone, it could never be rebuilt. She hadn't heard back, but if everything was okay, she hadn't expected to. It was the island way.

"I have a friend coming."

Why had she said that? It was none of Jeff's business. He wouldn't be interested, in any case. He was just a delivery service, dumping her on her rocky outcropping, and then he'd be back to his lobster pots and earning his living like an islander should.

She knew, though. She was diverting the conversation. It surprised her he didn't ask about her friend.

"Up?" The float shifted again. Jeff held her bags

and nodded toward the ramp, his feet moving that direction.

"Oh, right." She touched him on the shoulder. "Let me get one of those."

"I think you have enough baggage to carry already." He didn't turn, but he did pause for a moment. "Let me get this, and you try to leave the rest here on the float."

Katie stood frozen as he moved ahead. Had he really said that to her? And, God forbid, had she heard a smile in those words? Was he laughing at her? She wanted to call out, Just who do you think you are? The moment of rebuttal was gone, though, as he was half up the ramp and leaving her behind.

"Is my cabin still there?" She called to him as she looked up the ramp. It was across the Point on an isolated cove, and they would have to hike to it.

"Yes, ma'am, it is, at least until the next storm. What say you come along and we'll try to find it?" He set one of her bags down and reached to the rope to jangle the bell several times. He turned to look at her and laughed. "I remember you doing that every time I rowed up to your grandmother's float."

Katie remembered, too, although only after he reminded her. That last summer the bell had been her way of telling the entire island that Jeffrey Ragsdale had come to see her. Now it reminded her of the years it had been silent, and all that she'd lost so long ago.

Jeff had already turned, though, picking up the bag, and heading out of sight down the dock. She stood with one hand on the rail, closing her eyes for a moment. She couldn't go back. She couldn't afford to let herself go back. Not ever. She had to be strong.

The distant clang of a sea buoy caught her attention, and she focused on it, looking out towards the open water. Off in the distance the ferry plied the waves, returning to the mainland to pick up another set of intrepid seafaring islanders, either that or day-trippers come to enjoy the summertime delights of island life, imagining that it was really theirs to claim forever.

Seals, she thought. There should be seals. I used to see seals in the Cove, and I need to see seals.

That made her laugh at herself. Fourteen years gone, everything changed, and she wanted to see seals. What did seals have to do with anything?

She knew, though. The seals were always there, a thing that could be trusted. As long as the seals came to Rockhaven, then life would continue. It was permanence she needed, and the seals were that. The seals meant empty foundations and faded teenage crushes didn't matter so much. The seals meant she could go on, and all because they went on.

"Seals," she yelled at the empty ramp. "Where are the seals?"

The answer echoed back at her, "At the cabin," and she laughed. She truly laughed. Of course he would say that. Growing up, they'd always gathered at the cabin to watch the seals. And the whales. And the occasional dolphin. Of course the seals were at the cabin.

How could she have forgotten something as obvious as that?

3

"So, what is this? The scenic tour?"

They had followed the shore path rather than directly up the hill by Carver House. It was three times the distance, and there were several times they'd had to duck under low-hanging branches.

"I thought you'd appreciate missing what's missing." Jeff glanced at her out of the corner of his eye, and he winked. "If you get what's missing from what I'm not saying."

"My grandmother's house." The pain cut: the hugs upon her arrival each summer, the pies enjoyed, and the love she'd sensed so strongly nowhere else.

"Smart girl. Best not to be reminded of what's missing. Better to be reminded of what's at your side."

"Like you?" She couldn't believe she said that, but she couldn't take it back now, could she? And yet, with her words she felt her grandmother's ache ease into the background.

"Among other things. We're here. You go ahead." He stepped to the side of the path and nodded with his head. "It's yours. You deserve to be first there."

With him holding her bags, and the overhanging trees, it would be tight, but there was room for her to squeeze by, if barely.

"I deserve to be first, do I?" She took a deep breath. Fourteen years gone. Did she want to be there at all? Oh, she did, or she wouldn't have come, but what evil monsters was she opening the door to? There were a lot under there, too, ones she had barely buried all those years ago.

"Do you still see Ritchey and Janine?" She didn't move forward, and she knew her question for what it was. She was putting off seeing the cabin. If it were falling in, she would be heartbroken. If it weren't, she would be very surprised. A decade and a half wreaked havoc on abandoned island buildings.

"Ritchey and Janine?" Jeff laughed and threw his head back. "Yeah, Janine's still on island, but Ritchey? He got a degree at A&M. Said Texas was as cold as he ever wanted another winter to be, and he wasn't coming back."

"Never?" Ritchey had been Jeff's best friend, inseparable that last summer the boys were fifteen.

"He lied. Once, with his new wife. She complained of the boat rides every time they went into town. I think Ritchey let that be his excuse to abandon us forever."

Us. She heard that. Did us mean us, the islanders, or us, Jeff and her? Was she still a part of the island anymore, or just a tripper, come to soak up the summer's best, then go home to remember how wonderful life could be?

"Poor Ritchey." She smiled as she said it, though. "I'll need to get with Janine while I'm here."

"Four kids, the oldest eleven? Think about that before you call her up. All four are hellions, and I mean that with a capital H. Trust me."

"And you weren't?" They were teasing, like old times, and Katie felt herself slipping back into the familiar rhythms of easy interactions, like the time one of her seals had been sunning on the Carver House float, and when she'd come to take a picture, it had slipped into the water without a sound or ripple.

"I weren't. I was a good boy." He nodded down the path. "I've got your bags, still, and they aren't getting any lighter. If you'll move ahead."

"Sorry. Sure." She touched him on the arm as she stepped past, just enough to make sure he kept his distance from her. A branch caught in her hair, and she ducked lower, attempting to pull it free.

"Here."

She heard a bag drop, and she knew Jeff was untangling her hair from the branch. When he said, "There. All good," she stepped forward, murmuring, "Thanks."

When she emerged from the overgrowth, she felt her heart stop. In that pivotal moment, all her years of mainland life faded away. It was the summer she'd turned fourteen, with all the specialness of life on Rockhaven Island rolled in.

The stone path, half of exposed island granite, and the rest revealing odd-shaped stone pieces carried in one at a time and now surrounded by mossy soil, meandered toward the shore. Giant spruce rose up on the island side, and wild roses blanketed the seaward outcropping. Sheltered down the hill, just at the edge of the water, was her cabin, with shingled walls weathered to gray, the wooden roof brown and mossy with age, and wild ferns and white turtlehead along the foundation. Beyond stretched the sea, with a glimpse of Dyer's Rock to the left and Spurgeon Light to the right. The rush of water against the rocks whispered memories that carried her back to a happier time.

"Beautiful, I know. It's not changed, has it?" Jeff's voice brought her back to the moment.

Katie got herself under control. It hadn't changed, and that was what was wrong. Even the trim was painted a neat and orderly white, and it should be weathered and peeling. No paint lasted so long in the harshness of brutal island winters and blistering summer days.

"It's too perfect." She snorted at that, hoping he got her question. How was it too perfect? That's what she wanted to know.

"Think your friend will enjoy it?"

There was the laugh again, wrapped up in his words. His question told her more, though. He hadn't missed her comment from before. That was the boy she remembered, one who wove himself in and out of others' conversations, at ease with skipping his attention over the surface of whatever was going on, and never missing anything. It seemed that hadn't changed.

"Anyway," he continued, "I can see you already do. Go ahead. See if the inside's changed much."

"You're having fun with this, aren't you?" She glanced at him, not sure if she was amused or not. She wanted to be, if she could just figure out what was going on. The dock, the path, and now this? Not after years of disuse, it shouldn't be like this. She wanted it to look like this, but it shouldn't. It should be abandoned, like her feelings had been all those years ago. Then she could clear it all away, make it new, and make herself new in the process. This, though? This didn't allow her to change at all. Instead, it made her a teenager once again, and that was very bittersweet. She couldn't have one without the other, and the second half of her fourteenth year hadn't been memorable, not in a good way, anyway.

"Yes, I am." The laughter again, as Jeff answered her question. "Besides, I'm still holding your bags."

"Let me take one of those." She reached and grabbed the handle, only to find the side of her hand was now pressed against his. "Please?"

"How can I refuse please?" Still the laughter in the words. He released the handle.

"Thank you." She caught her breath and let out a long sigh. "Follow me that-a-way, sailor boy." She stepped down the path, the sweetness of moss and crushed clover rising with every step she took, letting herself be drawn into the picture.

"Sailor boy?" His voice was just behind her.

"You like bellboy better? I can give you a tip, then." With her free hand, she pushed her hair back from the side of her face and turned to him. As she did, she caught the sun glinting off the water, and she stopped, looking out to sea. "I remember this. Where have I been for half my life? Oh, this is beautiful."

"I know. I ask myself that question every day."

"You've been here every day. What do you have to miss?"

"You are something else." He grinned. "Every question you ask is exactly the one in my head. You and me? We're on the same page all the way."

Katie shook her head. She didn't know what page Jeff Ragsdale was on, but she'd closed that book long ago. He was on her page for today, but only by accident. Get her bags settled in, and she wouldn't need to see him again. She had her cell phone, a portable solar charger in her bag, and the number for Dyer's Delivery ready to go.

Yeah, Jeff, she thought, as she turned toward the cabin. What could you possibly have missed? You had the island all this time. You had everything I didn't. It was when she stepped onto the deck, swung the screen aside, and opened the cabin door that her underpinnings were blown wide. What she saw inside wasn't what she expected, by any measure.

Katie took in the cabin, but that meant she couldn't take it in at all. She stepped in and dropped her bag on a rush-bottomed bench at the foot of the bed, and she laughed.

"You don't like it?" Jeff followed her inside, setting the second bag on the floor beside the bed.

"What's there not to like?" She turned as she looked over the room.

That's all it was, too, a simple one-room cabin, with exposed studs and open rafters; and every wall filled with double-hung windows. The chest she remembered, hand-painted French, brought over by her grandmother from her native homeland. It had endured nearly a century of abuse by Katie and who knew who else, but it was pretty, still. The bench was one she'd picked out at an island tag sale when she was eleven.

The chair and desk facing the water had been a grandfather's she didn't remember. The bed, though. It was a queen, at least, with cream-colored linens; a thick comforter and matching dust ruffle; and four plump pillows. It had been two twins before. One for her, and the other for her friend Winnie Catron due on the first ferry in the morning.

"The bed, it's just a blowup." Jeff lifted the corner of the comforter to expose a hard plastic base with plastic legs. Above it was a quilted mattress. "The mattress looks real, but I had to blow it up with a hand pump."

"A hand pump?" She teased him. It seemed the culprit for all this was coming out.

"It's got an electric one, but I didn't think of that. Out here, no electricity. If it goes down—" He pushed on the top of the bed, his face turning red. "—it'll have to be hand pumped again."

"Oh, my!" She pushed on the bed, then sat on it. It was quite comfortable. "Are you going to come running when I call in the middle of the night? Hey, bell-boy, I need my mattress pumped up?"

"I should have planned it better." He brushed his face with his arm and took a deep breath.

"I shouldn't tease. I'm sorry. You did this?" She stood and walked to the windows facing the water. They were open to the sea breeze, and she chuckled. They were clean, too. Of course, he had.

"Um, well, Marc knew I always kept an eye on the place. Squatters, you know. They see a place empty, and they think they can just move in. So, I came out

28

from time to time to give the cabin a presence." He was still on the opposite side of the room.

"Come see this." She tapped the glass. "What's that out there?"

"The Lil' Dude, if I'm not mistaken." He was at her side. "With you coming, I thought you might like to see her out at the mooring."

"My Lil' Dude?" She felt the excitement rising. Lil' Dude was her sailing skiff, a white twelve-foot catboat, to be precise. She'd learned to sail her at nine, and she and Jeff had explored the coves, inlets, and nearby islands with as many people as they could pile aboard. They'd tipped her a few times, too, but that had been part of the fun, if they'd only thought so afterward.

"The same." He sounded pleased.

"You." She looked at him, unable to keep the smile from her face. "Now I can sail to town for groceries. I want to go out and see."

"You gonna swim out?"

"Swim?" She'd done that once at thirteen, but it made her think. "Where's the skiff?"

"Tied to the tree. Go see." He opened the door for her.

Down the gravel beach, there was a small boat, not over eight feet, just out of the water. A rope ran up over the rocks where it wrapped the base of a giant spruce.

"That's not my skiff." She walked across the gravel, calling back, "Where did this come from?"

"An extra. Yours was damaged the first winter you

were gone. Nobody remembered it down here, and it was broken up when my dad and I came to check on things that spring. Sorry."

"It's plastic?" She tapped the hull and laughed. "A plastic boat? How brilliant is that? It'll never rust, and it can't leak. Where'd you get this? Bean's?" She reached in and pulled out an oar. It was made of plastic, too.

"Lots of people have these now. Just don't forget to tie it up. Want to row out and see the Dude?"

"Of course I do. Life jackets?"

"Oh, yeah." Jeff stepped into the trees and returned with two orange jackets. He tossed them into the bottom of the boat. "That's taken care of. So, are we off?"

Another thing Katie had forgotten, the wooden locker in the trees. It held life jackets, spare rope, and at one time, even dry towels that her grandmother insisted be changed out every Sunday evening. What else had she forgotten from her distant past?

She didn't get to worry over it, though, because Jeff had the line loose, and he slipped the small boat back until all except the bow was on the water. He held it while Katie climbed inside, then he gave it a shove and leaped in after her.

"Hey!" She grabbed the side of the boat. It rocked seriously sideways before Jeff found his seat. "Careful, big boy."

"I thought it was bellboy." He clipped one oar in, then the other. Pulling, the small boat began moving toward the white sailboat moored in the cove.

"Big boy, bellboy, sailor boy, just get me there

high and dry. I don't have a washer. Remember, it burned up over a dozen years ago. It's hand wash while I'm out here this trip."

Then she could see the stern of the boat and the words written in the block script she remembered so well. Lil' Dude. The name had been hers. Her idea, anyway. She and Jeff, and probably Ritchey, had gotten a can of paint that first summer, and pulling the boat up on the float, Jeff had sketched the letters out with pencil, then laboriously, they had filled in the words one painstaking stroke at a time.

The letters were still fresh and perfectly sharp.

"Did you do this, too?" They were coming up beside the catboat, and she grabbed a varnished gunwale. That, too, was perfect. It hadn't been perfect the last time she'd seen it. It had borne five years of harsh, preteen use, and the "crew" hadn't been kind. Someone had put some elbow grease into her.

"My dad and me. We knew you'd be back some day, so we took care of her." He sounded proud.

"Your dad, how is he?" She remembered a weathered version of the way Jeff looked now. Gruff, but then that was the way of island men. The sea and long winters made them that way. The island hadn't turned Jeff, it didn't seem, but then maybe it had, and she was seeing him as she remembered him, rather than as what he was.

"Four years ago, we had an ice storm. It killed power to Otter's Reach." He was tying up to the mooring, and it seemed that was all he had to say.

"Your dad was helping?" She prompted him,

31

watching his strong hands working the line, loop-loop-and-under. When he looked up, she understood what had happened.

"They needed him, and he went. He never came home." His eyes were red, but he shrugged and smiled. "That's my dad. Stuff happens, and you go on. Now, onto your yacht, Dame Carver."

"I *am* going to push you overboard." She gave his shoulder a shove as she stepped into the Lil' Dude, laughing when the small dinghy rocked dangerously. "It's your own fault if you fall in, you know."

"And it's your own fault if I take you in with me. Let's go for a sail."

He leaped into the Dude, light-footed as Katie remembered him all those summers ago, and he landed with the preservers in one hand.

"For you," he handed her one, "and for me." He dropped his at his feet.

"Take me out, Captain." She smiled, enjoying the breeze and the memories of good times forgotten. She waved her hand at him permissively as he stood at the mast untying the sail.

"Thank you, Katie," he said. "I think I will."

She heard his words, and she heard her name. It was the way he said it, as if she had given him more than just permission to sail her boat. She groaned inside. What had she promised herself? Just this one day, and she didn't have to see him again?

She hoped she hadn't just tied an anchor around her heart, one that would sink her when it was time to leave the island. And she would leave. She had no place to stay, not for more than a weekend, anyway. All that had been stolen from her over a dozen years ago.

As she took the line from Jeff and looped it through a pulley on the stern, the wind caught the sail, and the small boat surged forward. Grinning, Jeff dropped beside her and took the line, pulling it taut, and sending the boat flying. It was wonderful to be back on the water, but Katie couldn't help but wonder, how would it feel when it all came to an end? Everything did. Nothing was forever, especially the things she loved the most.

If not for that reminder, her day out sailing in her prized and much-loved sailing skiff would have been absolutely perfect, the sort of day most people wished for and never got.

It had taken Katie fourteen years to get it back, and now, she wasn't sure just how it was going to end. Once they hit open water, it was the spray that made her forget all that. The boat leaped over a swell, and when it came down, the shower of sea water flew over the boat, dousing them both.

"Jeff, no!" she cried. "I can't get wet!"

"Sorry, Dame. Already done."

He was laughing, and she couldn't be angry. She was laughing, too. She let her self-control relax just a bit. Today, she told herself, just for this one afternoon, I won't wish for it to be over. I'll just enjoy myself as much as I can.

She was home, after all. She had been away too many years, and she had finally returned. For that, she could give in for just this one fun and irresponsible afternoon.

Real life could come calling later. It always did, one way or another. Just not while she was out in the Lil' Dude.

The Lil' Dude was meant for fun, and that's what she intended to have.

5

"Winnie! Winnie, Winnie, Winnie!" Katie squealed with excitement only to hear her own name yelled back at her.

"Katie! Katie, Katie, Katie!" Winnie Catron was exiting the ferry, and she dropped her two cases and raised her arms overhead to wave them back and forth. The man behind her was talking into his phone, and he barely avoided tripping over the abandoned luggage.

Katie grinned as her friend apologized profusely to the man—probably much more than precisely necessary—before yanking her far-too-large luggage out of the way and running clumsily her direction on too-high heels.

"Winnie! You made it, finally!" Katie threw her arms around her friend.

"Sweetie, I couldn't *not* make it. Too bad I

couldn't bring my car over. I'm mad at you about that, you know. These bags, whew!" She turned one on its side, and sitting on it, she worked one of her shoes off. "And these, not a good idea for that boat out there. Did you know it goes up and down the entire time it's moving? Can't they pick the smooth spot to drive on? I'm not getting on another boat until I leave this island, you can bet your bottom dollar."

Katie could see the problem. Her friend's shoes had six inch spikes, with straps that wrapped the ankles. At least no one would miss seeing them. They were neon blue. However, there was another issue, and she thought she'd better address it right away.

"Honey, I don't think that's possible." Katie grimaced at what she knew was coming. After all, she'd barely convinced her friend to join her. Family estate; summer vacation; you owe me this; she'd pulled out all her favor cards to convince her friend to tag along. And now she thought she wasn't getting on another boat until she left the island.

"You don't think what's possible?"

"The boat thing." Katie grabbed the handle of one of the cases and extended it, glad they put wheels on them. They had a ways to walk back into town. And they were walking. The parking lot was emptying as she spoke. If they waited much longer, they'd be the only ones in sight.

"So, where's our taxi?" Winnie had her shoe back on, and she stood, pulling her own case up and popping out the handle. "And I need somewhere to do my hair. It's out of control."

"Out of control?" Katie laughed. "Honey, your hair is never under control." If anything, her friend's hair was bigger than she'd ever seen it, an exuberant strawberry halo only tamed by two giant blue combs that matched her shoes.

"Anyway," Winnie sniffed, "about that taxi. I'm ready to get to the manor house. I need some R and R after that little boat ride over here."

"You want to stop in town and get a lobster roll?" Katie had begun making her way out of the parking lot by then, and Winnie was following. She hoped to get as far as possible before she had to reveal all her bad news.

"A lobster roll?" Winnie slapped one leg and hooted. "A lobster roll? What a punch line! Now tell me the joke. What is it, something like, how does a lobster get off a mountain? He does the lobster roll?"

"Don't be silly. It's a sandwich. We need to get something to eat before we head out to the house." Really, they did. She had yet to pick up any food. Breakfast this morning—in town, thank you very much— had been truly breaking a fast. She'd gone without eating since boarding the ferry the day before.

"I'll get a sandwich when we get to your grandma's."

"The kitchen is, um, has limited facilities. There." They had made it to Main Street, and Katie pointed to a little take-out window. "That's the local sandwich joint. They have fried chicken, too. My treat." She held up her pocketbook and waved it in the air.

"Sweetie, what did you do to your nails?" Winnie

grabbed her hand and held it still. "I know these nails did not rip themselves off without your help. Clams. Have you been digging for clams or something?"

"The ferry driver hit a rough patch in the road, and I forgot my file. I just haven't chewed them even, yet." She shook her hand loose. "Lobster roll or fried chicken?"

Winnie shrugged. "Taxi's my choice, but if you insist, I'll roll the dice. Get it? Roll the dice?"

"I get it." Katie rolled her eyes. She stepped up to the window. "Two lobster rolls with drinks and fries."

"Sauce?" came the reply.

"Sure," she said before handing over her money and collecting her change. "We'll be here at the tables." There were four picnic tables lining the street. Winnie was already parked with her shoe off again.

"We'll bring it out." The girl smiled and waved Katie away.

"Not much to it, is there?" Winnie called to her. "I mean, it's pretty and all, in a *Perfect Storm* sort of way, but who would want to live here?"

"Keep your voice down." Katie slid in next to her. "All these people want to live here. Me? I lived here every summer until I was fourteen."

"Oh, you poor sweetie! No wonder you are like you are!" Winnie put her hand on Katie's arm and clucked in a reassuring manner.

"Stop that!" Katie shook her off. "Wait till we get out to the Point. You'll see how beautiful all this is."

"So, tell me. Your grandma's house. Is it rebuilt?" Winnie's eyes sparkled. "You showed me those pictures. I imagine it brand new, with white clapboards, and a grand piano in the living room. Maybe a jetted tub in the bath. Could I ever use a jetted tub about now. And a feather mattress. That would make that boat ride out here worth it."

"We have to discuss that feather mattress." Katie was interrupted by the arrival of their food, and she spread it out between them. "Here, one Harbor View lobster roll deluxe, and one caffeine-spiked soda, for your island enjoyment."

"All right, I cave. This actually looks good. Coming in I thought I saw a white steeple. Is that church for Sunday?" Winnie took a sip of her drink, and then she bit into her sandwich. She wiped mayo from the corner of her mouth and smiled. "Oh, never mind church. I'm already in heaven. Thank you, Jesus, for bringing me heaven on earth, right here with my good friend Katie."

"Thank you, Winnie. With that sacrilegious talk, I'm making sure to have you in church on Sunday. Maybe even Sunday school." She grinned. If anything, her friend was more faithful than she was. Now, though, she eyed her friend's cases. Two of them, and they were very big. Too big to get back to the Point. Way too big.

"So," Winnie crumpled her paper wrapper, "I'm finished. Do you want to call the taxi, or shall I?" She pulled out her cell phone and held it up. "What's the number?"

"Call all you want." Katie reached and pushed the cell phone to the top of the table. "No taxi's taking you to Carver Point."

"No? I'll pay double. Else how'll we get there?" She tapped her phone. "Siri, find me a local taxi." She smirked in satisfaction.

"So, what's the number?" Katie peered at the phone's screen. She knew what it'd say. This was an island. A very small island. How many taxi companies did her friend think did business on an island?

The response finally came through. "Dyer's Delivery is all I can find, open Monday, Wednesday, and Friday. Would you like to schedule a delivery tomorrow morning?"

"What?" Winnie shook the phone. "Has Siri gone stupid or something? Okay, here I go again. Siri, find me—"

Katie covered her phone with her hand. "Honey, that *is* the taxi company. It's a boat, and it only runs three days a week. The other two it's over on East Haven, our sister island. Sorry."

"No taxi?" Winnie shook her head back and forth, setting her hair vibrating in the sun. "You brought me to a place with no taxis?"

"Not much else, either, I'm afraid. Those are very big suitcases. Do you need them both at the house tonight?" She refused to say cabin. Winnie needed the bad news metered out in very small doses.

"I packed light." Winnie huffed. "My blow drier and hair care supplies, along with my electric blanket." She tapped one of the cases with a smug smile. "See? I was paying attention. You said it might get cold at night. Oh, and extra shoes for Sunday. And in this

40

case," she tapped the other one, "fresh clothes for each day, and I brought a few movies and my tablet. You do have WiFi, right?"

"Ri-ight." Katie drew out the word and rolled her eyes. She hoped Winnie took the bad news well. She didn't have a bed for her to sleep on, not a real one, anyway.

"Is this seat taken?"

Katie froze. She knew that voice. She caught Winnie's eyes, to see her grinning and pointing with a poorly concealed finger behind Katie.

"No, this seat is not taken." Katie called her response without looking. She had looked yesterday and given in. Today? She was avoiding that pitfall at all costs.

"Good. The busboy needs to sit." Jeff did, and he slid a plate of fried chicken tenders onto the table. "I see you two ladies had takeout. I prefer the dine-in plate, even if I take it out."

"Ooh, Katie. You know this man?" Winnie's words were buttery, and she winked. "If so, you can introduce me anytime."

"Winnie, Jeff. Jeff, Winnie, my friend here for the rest of the week." She still refused to look.

"Winnie." Jeff held his hand over the table to shake. "Katie told me about you, and it was all good."

"Oh?" Winnie's face brightened. "That's different. I'm glad to meet you, Jeff." She reached back and took his hand, holding it definitely longer than was precisely necessary.

Katie kicked her under the table before she let go.

After their sailing expedition, she had sent Jeff on his way, showing him her phone and solar charger, that and the number for Dyer's. With the Lil' Dude, she'd chirped, she'd be fine on her own, so he needn't give her another thought.

She'd been fine for about three hours. Then she'd climbed between the sheets in her newly-made bed, and all she'd been able to think of was Jeff tying the knot on the mooring, Jeff reaching to untie the sails, Jeff laughing as spray doused them repeatedly. She could have had that, she knew, a lifetime of years ago. Now he was a fisherman, she had her Boston life, and she wasn't an island girl any longer. They could pretend, but they could never put back together what had been stolen from them.

By the time she'd thrashed herself to sleep, she'd blamed her parents, herself, and God. And she'd vowed she'd go out of her way to avoid Jeff the whole time she was on the island.

Now he'd found her out. This was not the place she needed to be at this time.

"So, for the third time, Katie Carver, how long have you known this handsome hunk?"

Katie blinked. For the third time? Where was her brain? And hunk? She blurted out before she knew what she was saying, "Hunk? Are you sexist? Good heavens, Winnie. He's just a boy I knew when I was a kid. Give me a break."

She stood and turned away. She still hadn't looked at him. She couldn't, not and walk away, and she had to walk away. She had to.

"I can move to a different table."

It was his voice. The same voice that had teased her the day before, the same voice she'd laughed with and that had made her feel so good. Would he haunt her entire week on the island?

God, why send him my way after all these years?

"No, you can't. I don't know anything about you, and you know all about me. It's not fair for you to leave now."

Katie knew *that* voice, too. It was her friend who would soon be her so-called friend if she kept butting in.

"Stay, Jeff. The lobster disagreed with me, and I need to catch some air. Winnie, toss the trash when you're finished." She reached for her wallet only to find empty table, and she cringed at having to turn and find it. Her eyes were burning, and she didn't dare let Jeff see. Then, someone slid the wallet under her fingers, just for moment touching her skin to skin before pulling away.

"Later, Katie, maybe?" It was Jeff again.

"Sure. Maybe. Thank you." She hadn't kept the quaver out of her voice that time, and she fled, walking across the street and through the town parking lot to stand at the water's edge.

The town was spread before her, hugging the rocky shoreline. Many of the shorefront dwellings had colorful shutters, some with contrasting doors. A number wore white clapboards, with just as many covered with weathered shingles. Summer boats of all sorts were attached to moorings leading toward the mouth of the harbor. It was so idyllic, she could not imagine she had stayed away her entire adult life.

She felt her control break. Why, why, why, God? How can I forgive you for what you took from me? This was mine, and then it was gone. Now you tease me with that man back there. It's not fair.

"Sweetie, are you okay?"

She felt an arm across her shoulders, and she straightened her face. She couldn't do anything about her burning eyes, but she could put on a good show. "Hey. I guess it's my hay fever. It gets me on the island every summer." She sniffled her best hay fever sniffle, and she laughed, hoping it didn't come across as too forced. "I should have brought my inhaler."

"Well, we're all taken care of. I told Jeff you were worried about my cases, and he said he'd bring them out. Sweetie, I don't know what bad blood there is between you two, because he seemed really sweet, but I know an old wound when I see one. You need me more than I thought. I'm here for you, no matter what, for the rest of the week. I won't leave your side." Winnie spoke softly and patted Katie's arm the entire time. "Remember, God loves you no matter what flowed under all those long-ago bridges."

"Sure. God loves me. I'll keep telling myself that. See that boat down there?" Katie pointed at the town float below where they stood.

"Which one, Sweetie?"

"The white one. It says Lil' Dude on the back end."

"Sure, that little bitty one. What a cute little toy.

What about it?"

"That's our taxi ride home." Katie felt her eyes well up. First Jeff, and now having to tell Winnie this? How bad did she have to feel before God quit squeezing her heart in his hand?

Winnie took a deep breath and let it out. "Okay, Sweetie, if you say so. Jeffie told me I might be riding back on a little bitty boat, no thanks to a warning from you. At least it's a cute one. Shall we get started?"

"Oh, you are a good friend." Katie gave her friend a big hug, even ignoring the mass of hair that got in her way. "I wouldn't trade you for anyone."

"I hoped you'd say that. Right now I'd trade you for a taxi with real wheels, though. How 'bout that?"

"Oh, you!" Katie pushed her friend away. "I'm sorry about that. The last time I was here there was a road to the house. It's impassable now. Everything becomes overgrown almost overnight. You really don't mind riding out with me? That's the boat I learned to sail on when I was nine."

"Sure! That's makes it even better. I'm scared of a boat even a nine-year-old can sail. What can be worse than that? Oh, and your Jeffie is gone. You can turn around now."

Katie frowned at that. Jeffie? Her Jeffie? Somebody had to be straightened out, and it had to happen soon, just not before she got Winnie onto that boat. This might be a trip to scare the devil out of a person, or Jesus into them. Dear God, she breathed. Please let this be the easiest trip I ever made.

After all, if He couldn't answer the hard prayers,

maybe He would give in and answer an easy one. Besides, this was for Winnie's sake, not hers.

For Winnie, please God? For Winnie's sake?

Then she remembered. Before they sailed away, they had to have food, and the store was right behind them.

"Honey, want to go shopping with me?" She smiled at her friend.

"Oh, Sweetie, I thought you'd never ask. I adore shopping!"

I bet you do, thought Katie. I really bet you do.

6

Katie had forgotten about the tides.

Her excuse was fourteen years off island. No matter her reason, the result was a wild fight once they approached the little cove in front of the cabin. The tide tugged the Lil' Dude one way, and Katie fought to force her another, the way of the mooring where the little dinghy was tied.

Poor Winnie wailed the entire time.

"We're going to die!" Winnie had her head between her knees, and her face was green in the gills.

"No, we're not. Keep your head down." That was important, too, because tacking repeatedly meant the sail had to swing to port, then to starboard, then back again, even as Katie forced the rudder left and right to offset the push of the wind.

Equally hard was keeping the small craft upright

with a dead body, er, dead weight sitting next to her.

"Duck! We're almost there!" Katie threw the rudder to the side and yanked the canvas sail over Winnie's head.

"I am ducked! I can't go any lower! Oh, I'm going to die!"

"Hold this. Pull it tight." Katie pushed the line into her friend's hand and leaped forward. "I'm tying off. You survived, you know."

"I did?" Winnie looked up.

Katie had hold of the mooring buoy, and she was pulling the line from the bow and attaching it to the mooring, loop-loop-tuck. She grinned. She stood and bunched the sail next to the mast and began securing it. "Now we get to switch boats."

"Here, in the ocean?" A new level of green painted Winnie's face. "I, I might fall into the water. Oh, oh, oh! Something's in the water." Her eyes grew wide as she looked to the back of the boat and tracked something up the other side.

"A seal! Oh, Winnie, this is so wonderful. I knew there had to be seals!" Growing up, Katie had looked for them every year, and she never felt like she was on the island, really here, until she saw her first one, and here it was.

"Will it, oh, oh, it's back! Will it . . . turn us over?" Winnie held to both sides of the boat, and her knuckles were white with fear.

"Not if you sing to it. They like *Hush-a-bye Baby.*" Katie refused to roll her eyes, but she was tempted. Seals were the gods of the sea, and there was nothing better, at least not to her.

"Hush-a-bye baby, don't you cry . . . down in the meadow, with little round eyes . . ." Winnie tracked the seal, her voice high-pitched and whispered.

"Not exactly, but it's working." Katie grinned. "Keep it up while I move our groceries." It was helping her friend stay occupied, at least. She dropped four shopping bags into the little plastic boat, and then she motioned to her friend. "Now, before the big, bad seal gets us. Hurry, Winnie!"

"Oh, it's back! I have to keep singing. Hush-a-bye baby . . . oh, it's looking at me! Can it tell I don't know all the words?"

"I can tell you don't know *any* of the words." Katie held Winnie's hand, but she was over by that point. "Now sit so I can come over."

"Okay. Hush-a-bye baby, sweet little seal. I don't want . . . to be your next meal . . ."

"He's gone. You can stop, now." Katie snapped the oars in place and gave the line one last tug to free it. Then she pulled, and the boat surged slowly forward.

"Oh, he's following us." Winnie pointed. "Oh, oh! Hush-a-bye sealie, go go away . . ."

"He's your friend for life, Honey. You bewitched him with that voice." About then the little dinghy crunched gravel, and Katie snapped the oars loose and dropped them in the floor. "Sit still while I get out."

"Don't leave me!"

"With all our groceries? No way. Now hold still." She jumped over the bow, her feet crunching the wet stones, and she yanked the small boat forward. "Now, your hand, Honey. I'll help you out."

"Please. Oh, I've never been so scared in my life." Winnie grabbed Katie's hand and stumbled out of the boat, still in her blue heels.

"Me, either. I was out there with a mad woman."

"Who? I didn't see another boat anywhere." Winnie patted her hair, taking a deep breath and looking around. Back on solid ground, her color was quickly returning to normal.

Katie tucked her chin and looked at her friend. "Who? You have to ask who? Who was singing a bedtime song to a fish?"

"It was your idea, and a seal is not a fish."

"But you *were* singing." Katie grinned.

"And these are groceries. Can we talk about a refrigerator, and a stove, and maybe hot chocolate with mallows? Now, that's a good conversation." Winnie reached into the boat and looped the bags across her palm, lifting them up to hold them over her shoulder. "Is there anything else I can help you with, Sweetie?"

"Step out of the way. I have to tie up the boat." She yanked it across the gravel, barely missing her friend's legs, and causing her to jump sideways with a screech. "Don't be a baby. I missed you by a mile."

"An inch. You can pull that boat all by yourself?"

"It's just plastic. It's not heavy."

"Plastic?" Winnie kicked it with her foot. "You had me in the ocean in a plastic boat? That's dangerous! How could you?" She sniffled. "I should have ridden back with your nice Jeffie after all. He offered,

50

you know."

"Well, he's not my Jeffie, so it doesn't matter." Winnie had finally gotten on her nerves, and Katie let her cross feelings be heard. "I told you before, I knew him growing up, and I haven't seen him for fourteen years."

"Oh. Then it doesn't matter that he likes you." Winnie slipped out of her shoes and held them in one hand, with the bags still in the other. "Or did you even notice?"

"There's nothing to notice." Katie busied herself with a knot tying up the small boat. The thing was, she had noticed.

"Okay. I'll play your game. Well, that hunk you haven't noticed is coming out of that little building down the beach." Winnie pointed with the hand holding her blue shoes. "I think he's looking this way, and I think it's right at you. I bet he notices." She giggled.

"Heaven help me." Katie closed her eyes and shook her head. If Jeff was here, there was no way to avoid looking at him. Why didn't he just stay away? Oh, she'd forgotten. It was thanks to her friend who had packed two bags of electronics that were useless here on the Point.

"Katie! Winnie!" Jeff called to them, his hand in the air waving. "Or are we back to Dame Carver?"

"Don't you start, Jeff! I mean it!" Katie put her hands on her hips and glared at the raggedy-haired man standing on her deck.

"Dame Carver?" Winnie giggled again. "This is almost worth that boat ride out here."

51

"I dropped off your bags, and I left a few other things, too. I'll leave you two ladies to settle in. I haven't forgotten our lobster bake this weekend." He waved cheerily, and with a grin, he turned and took off running up the hill.

When he was gone, Winnie stepped to the water's edge and looked up and down the beach. She turned back to Katie with a frown. "No boat. Where's he going?"

"The dock's on the other side of the Point. He's probably over there. Trust me. Jeff can find his own way home." Thank goodness he had taken off, too. Then it hit her. A few other things? What things would he have left for them? "I want to see what he's been up to. Follow me." She motioned to Winnie and started toward the cabin.

"Not so fast. This place is cute." Winnie followed her to the deck and dropped her shoes before turning to take in the ocean view. "A lighthouse and everything. I can't imagine how super your grandma's house must be."

"Oh, my!" Katie had the door open by then, and she could barely get out the words.

"What's inside that's so special?"

"Lights." Katie laughed, and it was rather high-pitched and manic, even to her. "We have lights."

"That's special?" Winnie stepped up and peered over her shoulder. "Oh, this is so cute. Who stays here?"

"How can we have lights?" Katie stepped inside. There were two floor lamps, one on each side of the bed, both glowing with yellow electric light. "We don't have lights. I can't have lights."

"Sweetie, I hate to tell you this, but you do have lights. One, two. You can count them on two fingers." Winnie held up her hand, lifting one finger, then a second. "At least that's the way I learned in kindergarten."

"You don't understand." Katie moved to the far side of the bed to see a large plug box on the floor and pushed up against the wall, with an equally large black cord disappearing underneath the bed. "We never had electricity on the Point. Just candles and oil lamps."

"Well, these are the real things." Winnie looked under one shade. "Yep, glass bulbs and all."

"Shush!" Katie put her fingers to her lips. "What's that?" A low sound, one that shouldn't be there, made the floorboards vibrate. "Turn that light out." She flipped the one on her side of the bed.

"Whatever." Winnie shrugged and flipped the light off. The vibration stopped.

"Now, listen." Katie turned hers back on. The vibration started up again. "That's a generator, if I know my electricity."

"Okay, and that means?"

"It means I'm finding that generator." Katie stamped out the door and circled the little cabin. Sure enough, there in the shadowy darkness, resting on four blocks at the back of the building, was a little gasoline generator humming away. "Ooh, Jeff," she growled.

"Jeffie did this?" Winnie was at the corner of the structure with her arms crossed and her giant mane of hair silhouetted against the light coming off the ocean. "If that means I can run my curling iron, then he's a better man than you give him credit for. Yea, Jeffie!" She began to clap her hands.

"He wants something, that's all." Katie brushed past her to stand in the light. Why can't he not do stuff for me? she pleaded to God, if no one else. All she wanted was to be here for the week, try to find what she'd lost, and move on with her life. She didn't need mired in the past all over again.

"Like a lobster bake?" Winnie draped an arm around Katie and put her chin on her shoulder. She whispered, "What's so bad about a lobster bake? That sounds pretty good to me."

What was so bad about a lobster bake? Nothing, Katie thought, looking out to sea at the lighthouse, brilliantly lit on one side, and shadowed on the other. It's what's in the shadows that's the problem. It's feelings that I had to bury half a lifetime ago, and I don't know what might boil back up if someone scratches hard enough. She grabbed her friend's arms and squeezed them. Then she forced a laugh, pulling free and turning back to the cabin.

"This is it, you know. You keep asking about my grandmother's house, and this is all that's left. We get to share it for the week, just you and me." She was bright; and she stepped to the deck, threw back the screen door, and struck a pose. "Welcome, mademoiselle, to my humble abode. Underneath this roof is where we'll spend our time for our week on the island." Then she felt her face crack, and the tears began to flow.

"Sweetie, what?" Winnie reached to her to put her arms around her friend.

"I lied to you. Well, not lied, but I showed you those old pictures, and I let you think all that was still here. Well, it's not. It burned down a long time ago, and this is where we're staying. We don't even have a bathroom!" She began to sob.

"You got a tree?"

"A tree? There are tons of trees. How's a tree going to help?" Katie sniffled and wiped at her eyes.

"You got a tree, and that's all we need." Winnie giggled. "Well, not all, but we'll manage. We're women, after all. We can do this!"

"Thank you, Winnie. I'm being melodramatic, and I'm sorry. I can do better than a tree." Katie smiled at the idea of using a tree. Men, yes. Women, no. "There's an outhouse just down the path."

"Oh, then we're high style. An outhouse *and* electricity. What can be better than that?" Winnie primped her hair. "Now, where did you say the kitchen is? We've got groceries to put away."

Katie shook her head. "That's something else I didn't get a chance to tell you . . ."

7

"Jeffie" had been more than a "dear." In spite of herself, Katie had finally admitted that to Winnie. She had groused the whole time, though.

It was the tiny refrigerator that won her over, more than the lamps and even more than the folding bed they'd finally noticed nestled behind the door.

Now, though, Winnie's electric blanket was keeping both of them warm.

"Another one, there. See it, Winnie?" Katie pointed overhead. In the city-free sky, the stars were brilliant diamonds on velvet. There was a meteor shower in place, and they were snuggled up on the deck, trying to be the first to see each one.

"That's six for you, and none for me." Winnie pulled her tablet from under the electric blanket and tapped another checkmark by Katie's name.

"Just watch. They're there." Katie jabbed her finger at the sky. "There, I think. Maybe . . . no, maybe not." She giggled. "Sorry. That's an airplane. See the flashing light?"

"I don't know if any of them are real. I think you're making them all up." Winnie tucked the tablet back away and pulled the blanket tighter under her chin. "I mean, like, it's summer, and it's cold out here."

"It's Maine. What'd you expect? I love it like this."

"Oh, I guess I expected a big white house, a claw-foot tub, and maybe a footman and a scullery maid." She giggled. "I didn't get any of those, did I?"

"You got me." Katie pulled her friend's arm close and squeezed it.

"So, are you ready to talk?"

"Talk?" Katie suspected she knew what about. And no, she wasn't ready to talk.

"Come, girl. We've been friends for a hundred years, and you never told me you once had a boyfriend who looked like your Jeffie. Now I want to know everything. I deserve it after you tortured me with that boat ride out here."

"He wasn't a boyfriend. We were a pack of wild animals, prowling the dark undersides of the island." If she made a joke of it, it was easier to tell, and she laughed at the idea of the island having any dark undersides at all. It had been fun and adventure to her, trailing after Jeff and his friends all summer long.

"That just makes it better. Two don't make a pack.

57

Who else was there?"

"Besides me and Jeff? Janine. She's still on the island, and with four wild animals of her own, according to Jeff. Jeff's best friend Ritchey is in Texas. He said he needed to thaw for a few decades."

"Thaw?"

"Remember? Maine? You think it's cold now. It's summer. Try January and ten below."

"No thanks. I want the warm months only. Anyone else?"

Winnie really did sound interested, and the names began coming back to Katie. She told of them all. Apple Dumpling. They laughed, and Katie assured her friend that was really her name. She was conceived under an apple tree or something.

And Austie Williams, tall and lanky, the oldest of the bunch. Maybe a year older than Jeff, but with the presence of a high school boy. He wanted to be a pilot, but she had no idea what had become of his dreams. Yes, she could find out, but after so long, he wouldn't remember her, anyway.

The Reynolds twins were the pranksters. Bennie and Bobby, they wore matching shorts, and they'd switch shirts all day long, until no one knew which one was which. Heaven help them if they both married. Their wives would never know if they had the correct husband. Ritchey could always tell, but then Ritchey had an eye for faces that no one else did.

Babes Baker was the beauty of the bunch. A year younger than Katie, she'd gotten in trouble that final summer. Just a kid, her parents had sent her off island so no one would know. Maybe the adults hadn't clued in, but the gang all knew. It was Babes, and that meant it was obvious.

"How sad. Thirteen and saddled with a reputation." Winnie sat up, pointing. "There, I see one. A shooting star, and a big one."

"Good for you." Katie cheered her friend's success. "I told you they were up there."

"So, you and Jeffie. What was your connection back then?"

"There was no connection. We were part of the same pack, and at the end of the summer, we all went our separate ways, except the islanders, of course. They never talked about their winters here. Summer was summer, and that's what we were, summer friends."

"Oh, don't give me that. You said he's a year older. He must have been like a big brother, or a crush or something. You've got to tell me what it's about. Make it up, if you have to, but I want a juicy story."

"You're a hopeless romantic. That's your problem." Katie smiled. She had so admired the boy she'd known back then. And she had mourned when he was gone. She couldn't go through that again.

"Did you ever hold hands in the moonlight?" Winnie nudged her.

"Oh, you! We might have dug clams in the moonlight, but that's all, and trust me, there's nothing romantic about digging for clams, either in the moonlight or on a sunny day. It stinks, because the mud you dig in is the same mud they defecate in."

59

"Ooh! TMI, Sweetie. I'll never eat another clam again." Winnie visibly shivered.

Katie laughed. It served her friend right, probing for information she had no right trying to dig out of her past. Anyway, it was time for bed, and there was a nice, soft mattress calling. With the generator, she didn't even have to worry about phoning for a bellboy in the middle of the night. Jeff had hooked up the electric pump. She was going to be safely ensconced, wrapped up in her island dreams all night long.

"Okay, Honey, let's pack it in. Dawn comes early on the island."

"Sure." Winnie yawned. "How early?"

"Five-ish, right through these windows. Visit the potty if you need to. I have a flashlight."

"Five-ish, huh? What happened to seven-ish?"

"Move to Florida." Katie pulled the blanket to her and unplugged the cord. Absently, she began to fold it in half then half again. "You want this tonight?"

"Sure." Winnie took it. "You don't mind the foldaway?"

"Yes, I mind the foldaway very much. Good try." It was already set up with Winnie's things. They'd pushed the big bed to the side, and that left just enough space for the smaller one. It was the lack of blinds that was going to be the problem. There were none. The roll-down shades Katie remembered from her childhood had apparently rotted clean away. The hooks were there, but the shades were nowhere to be seen.

Happy sunshine in the morning! It would be, too, whether they liked it or not!

8

It was the smell of food that pulled Katie from her island dreams. Then, maybe the smell of food was part of her island dreams.

She pushed the covers aside, only to have a fragment of morning sun hit her in the face. The trees to the east were some protection, and moving her head sideways was all it took to find relief. The cold? It was freezing outside of the bedclothes. Only the midday sun would provide any relief for that.

"Winnie?" It really was food. She could still smell it.

"Umm." The sound moaned from under the tumble of electric blanket rumpled across the small bed. There was a click from the controller, and outside, the generator whirred on.

"I smell food. Have you been up?"

"Umm. Takeout, maybe." The mound moved, but no one came out, and the words were muffled.

"Via helicopter, if so." Katie pushed the covers aside and stood, finding her slippers for her feet. The floor was cold. She pulled an old pink terry robe around her, the one concession she'd made for the cool nights. She'd remembered how cold it got even on the warmest summer days, and it was worth the baggage space.

Out across the water, the top of the lighthouse was just catching the sun. The Dude was still in full shade. The cabin didn't catch the sunrise, and from here, she had always judged the time of day from the top of the lighthouse. She guessed five-forty, give or take fifteen. The thrub thrub of a motor floated across the water, the sound finding its way in through a window that hadn't wanted to close completely the night before. In the distance the wake of a lobster boat cut a path in the ocean.

"Island morning," she whispered as she yawned. "I still smell food."

"Breakfast?" A hand peeked out of Winnie's covers, the fingers wiggled, and it withdrew back into its shell.

"I sure didn't cook." Still, while the smells of cooking sometimes carried from houses across the cove on the south side of the Point, from this side? She'd never noticed it before. Then, she'd rarely over-nighted in the cabin, either, so maybe it was something that was always here, and she'd never been around to smell it.

She stepped to the door and pulled it open. The smell of spruce and pine and clover—and the barest continued hint of breakfast—surrounded her, and she smiled. "I'm stepping outside, Honey. Stay warm."

"Kay." The fingers wiggled again before disappearing. The control clicked, and the whirring from the generator died away, leaving the lapping of the water against the rocks as the only song of the morning.

Outside was where she found the cause of the smell. An insulated bag sat on the deck with a note attached to the handle. She turned it over to read, "Thought you might like a hot breakfast." Out of the bag came the wonderful smell of sausage, eggs, and muffins, just like Harbor View had served up on cool summer mornings all those years ago.

"Your fairy godfather's been by. There's hot food when you're ready." Katie stepped inside to set the bag on the desk before moving back to the deck. Stuffing her hands in her pockets, she removed her slippers and stepped to the rocks just off the deck. The tide was high this morning, and it lapped right at her feet. Down the beach, the little plastic dinghy floated at the end of its tether.

She wasn't happy. She knew where that food had come from, the same place as the generator, the extra bed, and the little fridge. She didn't intend to eat a bite of it, either. What made it worse was that she should be grateful. She wanted to be grateful, but she couldn't. Every little thing was like another string connecting her to a past she was desperate to forget, tying her down and refusing to let her go. She saw the checkmarks lining up in her head, a whole row of favors Jeff could call in. Each one made it more and more difficult to push him away. She didn't want to be in his debt. She didn't want to be in anyone's debt.

She found a spot where the sun hit her face, and she closed her eyes and pulled her arms around her. For a moment, she let the sounds and smells of the island push the painful connections away: her old summer friends, the house she hadn't yet found the courage to explore the remains of, and the God she had yet to forgive for not taking care of something that had been really important to her. None of that mattered; the important thing now was being here at this moment in time. The island was forever, like her seals, always the same, the waves returning hour after hour, just waiting on her to remember them.

Carver Point had waited, too, fourteen years. It had waited, welcomed her back, and wrapped its arms around her. It was the in between that got in the way.

"Look at you out there." The screen door opened and slammed.

"Hey. You're awake. Find your breakfast?" Katie didn't look.

"I'm eating it." Winnie crunched the gravel beside her, one hand wrapped around a partially eaten muffin sandwich, and the other holding her phone and doing something with her thumb. She held it in front of her, and the device made several clicking sounds. "There, got some pictures I can post. Took one of you. See?"

"In this old thing?" Katie looked, and sure enough, there she was, in her pink terry, looking out across the water, with the lighthouse in the distance. "Feel free to erase that."

"No way." Winnie wiggled the sandwich. "This is good. I liked the note. I guess, Jeffie?"

"Probably." Katie kept her tone even. Jeffie. Harrumph was what she thought. "Lobstermen get out early, and I guess he thought he was being kind. You know, your first morning. Eat it all, but don't expect it again." She would make sure of that. Anyway, when he realized she didn't want to see him, he would fade out of the picture fast enough. Silly summer girl, didn't even have a house or money anymore. She had nothing to offer him, and that wasn't going to change.

"Here." Winnie forced the uneaten part of her sandwich with its paper wrapping into Katie's hand. "It's cold out here, and I've got to visit the potty. Feel free to eat the rest of this. There's another back inside." Her footsteps crunched on the rocks twice, then the sound from her feet was swallowed up by the moss along the path.

Katie looked at the sandwich with its one bite missing. Steam rose from the still warm meat inside, and she felt her stomach rumble. Taking a bite, she let the warmth slide down her throat.

"This is good," she murmured. "Okay, *Jeffie*, just for this morning I forgive you. For not coming to find me all those years ago, I forgive you, because I am really, really hungry; and bringing this by was exactly the right thing for you to do."

She licked the fingers on one hand when she was finished, and she wadded the paper and held it tightly in her fist. She still couldn't figure out exactly why Jeff was doing all this. No one waits around fourteen years, and then picks up where they left off. No one, and she wouldn't believe it if anyone claimed it to her.

Anyway, she'd just been the summer tag-a-long, and he'd barely paid her any attention back then. Maybe he was sorry for her because of losing everything. Yeah, his dad was probably the reason. He remembered that, and that was why he was trying to make things easier for her.

Somehow that made her feel better, and when Winnie called to her from the path, she turned and waved. "I have something I want to show you. Come see."

"Sure. You still have my sandwich?" Winnie readjusted one of her blue combs as she walked across the deck, using it to pull her tresses from her face to form a halo at the back of her head.

"I have the wrapper. I couldn't resist. Look there." She pointed to the lighthouse. "The sun, it's halfway down the side. That's about six, July time. When it hits the rocks at the waterline, it'll be about six-fifteen. It's like my own personal sundial."

"Six? In the morning?" Winnie looked aghast.

"No, in the evening. Of course in the morning, you silly goose."

"This is awful! I'm going back to bed. I'm glad I brought my electric blanket." Huffing, Winnie marched back inside, letting the screen slam on the way in. Her voice filtered out, "Why does God make the sun come out at this time of the morning, anyway?"

Katie smiled. She didn't mind. She enjoyed island mornings, ones just like this. The Dude moved in a swell, and something onboard clanked, the sound carrying easily across the water. When she looked farther, the double tracks from the lobster boat were closer. She caught sight of the familiar shape of the vessel at the head of the tracks, smiling to see the lobsterman standing just outside of the wheelhouse, with one hand in the air. Then she narrowed her eyes. It was! She turned away. It was Jeff Ragsdale, out there spying on her, and proud to be doing it. He was waving at her, as if she should be excited to see him. Waving!

That was the final straw. All she had was this one little beach left to her name, and he was taking even that away. He'd better not show up for any lobster bake on her beach. She'd bake his little waving hands right in the coals, just to make her point.

She felt her eyes burn, and in her frustration, she tried to find fault in the scene before her: the cabin with its freshly painted trim, the walk, neatly trimmed, and the dappled sun through the trees falling across the roof of the cabin and onto the outer edge of the deck. As she stood there, the little gasoline generator kicked on, purring quietly in the morning air. The deck! Why hadn't she paid attention to that before? None of the boards were rotted. Not a one. How had that happened after being left to the weather for years and years?

Guilt wrenched her. She had to pay him back. That was it. Even if he'd done this for his father, she had to pay Jeff back, whatever it took to get the money to do so. If only the Rockhaven Carvers weren't as broke as a tree branch after a spring snow storm.

Rockhaven Carvers? Rockhaven Carver. There were no others. She was the only one left.

The overwhelming responsibility brought tears to her eyes, ones she didn't know if she could ever brush away.

9

"Have you started a love affair with that thing?" Katie lounged in the sun on a cloth and metal chaise. Next to her, Winnie hunched forward over a cell screen, occasionally tapping something only she could see.

"Sweetie, with anything that loves me back. It's why I like you so much." She smiled and kissed the screen. "We did it, girl! We're there!"

"Did what?" Katie's question was less of a question than verbal support for her friend. Right then, she would support almost anything Winnie did, just for these lounge chairs. When Winnie had pulled the first one from her biggest suitcase, Katie had shaken her head in dismay. Unfolded on the deck, she had changed her mind. Then, a second had appeared, its twin, and Winnie had become the best thing she could have possibly brought with her to the island.

"Got a hundred likes. See?" She held out the phone.

"Let me see." Katie shaded the screen, and it was dim in the bright sun, but there she was in her pink robe with Spurgeon Light in the distance. "Get real. No one would want to see that old picture."

"Not over a hundred people, anyway." Winnie snickered as she took back the phone. "That bumps you to the top of the list. Everyone'll see it now."

"Who would want to look at me?" Katie worked her fingers into her hair, and she pushed it back from her face. Winnie was the lucky one, with her vibrant head of hair. Sure, her friend complained she couldn't do anything with it because it was so coarse, but while she got its thick texture from her father, from her Irish mother, it was a beautiful strawberry blonde. Against her dark skin, it was stunning.

Katie knew *she* wasn't stunning. Not ugly, no, but not stunning, not to get calls for catalog modeling like the friend at her side. No, Katie depended on neatness, nicely manicured nails, and good manners to get her through. After all, she continually told herself, when your hair is board straight and your body is too, you'd better have a wonderful personality.

She wasn't sure she had mastered that this weekend.

"Oh, oh, there. Look-it that!" Winnie held the phone out again.

"Just tell me. The sun's too bright."

"Your Jeffie likes it, too." Winnie giggled.

"My Jeffie? Are you on Facebook?"

"Of course. Where else? It's how the world stays in touch. It looks like Jeffie wants to stay in touch, too."

"Give me that phone." Katie grabbed it and stood, walking over to stand under a tree. Shading the screen, she enlarged the image to read the comments underneath. She growled when she saw his name.

"You like-ee?" Winnie had a very pleased expression on her face.

"I do not *like-ee*. How is Jeff on your Facebook page?" She stalked back over and tossed the phone in her friend's lap.

"He's my Facebook friend, number, um," and she tapped on the screen, "1,203 out of 1,203. I looked him up yesterday and friended him. He friended me right back."

"You friended him." That took Katie aback. Winnie had friended him, and there he had been. Why had she never thought of that? What about Ritchey, Apple, Austie, and the others? How many of them were out there ready to be friended, and she didn't know?

"Sweetie, I friend everybody." Winnie held her hair out of the way and gave Katie a peck on the cheek. "Besides, I asked him yesterday if he had a Facebook account, and he asked me to friend him. See? Be friendly to the natives, and they'll be friendly to you. Are we going to town today? I want to watch another lobster roll down the mountain."

Katie looked, and Winnie's eyes sparkled with amusement. "You mean that?"

"Well, I can sit here and be beautiful all day, but there's only you to see. If you can keep from drowning me, I can be beautiful all the way to town and back again, and everyone will get to enjoy me." She smiled brightly.

"After your complaints yesterday, you must have an ulterior motive." Katie pursed her lips in thought. "I just can't figure out what."

"Isn't it obvious?" Winnie pulled up Katie's hand. "I looked for my nail file, and I can't find it anywhere. I can hardly file these down with a rock, can I? And I promise not to scream but a little bit."

"Okay. I get it. It's all about my broken nails." Katie pulled her hand away, pleased at her friend's concern, and aware of the smile on her own face. "And I promise to pay attention to the tides. That was the real issue yesterday. Today will be much better, I promise."

"I hope so, but just in case, I have a new background on my phone."

"9-1-1?" Katie thought that was funny.

"Better. Matthew 14:25. Jesus walked on the water." She held the phone up again. "That's what I'm going to do when you sink us, and then I also have Verse 31 for after we sink. Jesus saved everybody. See? I'm all set."

About then, the sound of the generator broke the quietness of the morning, and Katie questioned, "Winnie, did you turn your blanket off?"

"Of course, Sweetie. Why?" Her head was already back in her phone once again.

"It takes gasoline to run that generator, and it's running now. I don't know how long the fuel will last." Then she remembered the little fridge. It might have kicked on. "It's probably the refrigerator. I forgot about that." Katie sank back into her chair.

After a moment, she began to smell something. She sniffed. "Winnie? Is something burning?"

"Oh, that's me!" Winnie jumped up and handed Katie her phone. "The signal's not great, but feel free to play. My curlers are ready. See you in a bit!"

The screen slammed, and she was gone.

Katie stroked the slim wooden armrest on the folding chair with one hand and held the phone in the other. Glancing back in the cabin to see Winnie preoccupied with working giant rollers into her hair, she tapped the Facebook icon. Under the Friends section, she scrolled until she found Jeff's name. She felt guilty, like a voyeur, secretly peeping where she hadn't been invited. With her heart pounding she tapped on him.

There he was, his page, all the things he had posted for the world to see. Photos. She tapped and began to scroll. Rockhaven Town Church. There were lots of those, tag sales on the lawn, what seemed to be picnics and dinners on the grounds. Some of the same people were in a number of pictures at the quarry; the younger ones wore swimsuits, with one adult floating on a blowup ring in the water. What looked like parents were sitting on chairs to the side. She enlarged that picture, realizing it was Jeff on the ring. He was waving at the camera; it reminded her of her last summer

73

on the island, except he was wearing a black suit rather than cut-off jeans.

Scrolling further, there were more of Jeff: at the family home she'd visited once or twice out on Moffat Cove; several on a lobster boat she recognized as his dad's old one. He had his arm across his dad's shoulders in one, and he was laughing and holding up a live lobster.

Jeff kept getting younger as she went. He had on a Rockhaven High basketball uniform, and his hair was wet with sweat; he stood around a bonfire on the rocks, in shorts and athletic shoes but wearing a heavy jacket.

She almost passed the picture of her, going on before she recognized herself and went back. She looked at the image for a long time, the memories flooding back. She didn't know who had carried the camera, but Austie and Ritchey had cooked up a scheme to harvest clams to sell to trippers at the ferry terminal. They'd gotten the twins excited with all the money they'd make, but they'd needed a boat. The best mud flats were at the head of Carver Cove at low tide. Katie's little rowing dinghy was convenient, so she was roped in as the only girl on the expedition. Jeff had been enlisted to talk her into it.

They'd towed several long boards behind the boat to lay out on the mud. Otherwise they'd sink to their knees. In the picture, she was in the boat leaning over the bow with a long trowel in her hand. Mud smeared one cheek. One of the boards, mostly brown but sprinkled with flaking white paint, stretched to the side out of the picture. Jeff was on it, his arms covered with mud to his elbows. He was looking at the camera, and he held a giant clam up to show it off.

The camera had focused on Jeff. He was sharp and clear. His eyes sparkled with laughter, the flat planes of his face broken with his dimpled grin. He had pride written all over him.

Her? She looked up at Jeff, grinning stupidly. The color was faded a bit at the edges of the photo, as if it had been displayed in a window or on a wall, and the sun had worked its fingers over the image day after day. One corner had a little tear.

That was the moment she had known she was in love.

Just fourteen, there had been no doubt. During her childhood she had followed him, worshipped him, and wished to be an island child like him. She had never thought of it as love, although in retrospect, she didn't suppose she thought of it as love even that day. In that moment, just when that picture was snapped, everything in her life had taken on a different focus. That muddy boy digging for clams had seemed just about perfect to her. Who wouldn't fall in love with a muddy island boy with dimples the size of the Grand Canyon?

Then September had come calling, the bad news had come calling, and Jeff—her Jeffrey—hadn't come calling. She'd known that if she loved someone enough, he'd feel her need for consolation, and he'd come to find her, wouldn't he? And when he didn't, she'd trusted in a God who could do anything, even magic, as long as she believed in it. She had believed, and watched the phone, and checked her mailbox.

She clicked the phone off and turned it upside down. You can't have back what you never had in the first place. Just because one person falls in love doesn't mean the other person even knows. Does it?

And just because you ask God doesn't mean He answers, does it?

Well, she had picked up the pieces, and she had moved on. God still had a place in her life, but it was a carefully regulated one. After all, if He couldn't do what she had asked of Him, why should she go out of her way for Him?

She did envy Jeff in all those pictures with his Rockhaven Town Church friends. They seemed so happy together. If he had come to find her, she could have had that, too.

She closed her eyes against the sun and listened to Winnie humming inside and the soft slap of the water against the hull of the Dude. If the breeze picked up, Winnie might get quite a ride back into town.

The wind shifted, and she caught the clover and the roses, the fragrance wafting over her in waves. She didn't need Jeff and all the laughter in those pictures. She had this, and how could life get any more perfect than Carver Point?

It was a slice of heaven right here on earth.

10

"Are you sure about this?" Katie stood at the tree serving as an anchor for the plastic dinghy. The air was motionless where they were, but far out, the wind pulled white feathers from the surface of the water. Any location unprotected would be risky in a boat as small as the Dude.

"I can only post so many pictures of the same rock, Sweetie. Fresh air! Besides, I want to see what the coastline looks like."

"You just traveled it yesterday. It's not any different today."

"My head was between my knees yesterday. I didn't see any of it." Winnie had a bag across her shoulder, and she dropped it to the rocks and pulled out her phone. "Look at that. Seagulls. Hold a minute. I have to make a post."

Katie watched the Dude and the direction she pointed, still concerned. Follow the tide out, and later in the day, follow the tide back in. If Winnie knew how to sail, it would be manageable at any time, as long as they had wind. But, as she couldn't resolve that issue, tide out and tide in was very important.

Anyway, if push came to shove, they could tie up at the dock on Carver Cove and hike overland across the Point. It'd only save them about ten minutes sail time, but it would save them a lot more if they were blown all the way to East Haven.

The hike? That would add twenty minutes.

"Ready!" Winnie dropped her bag in the dinghy. "You want me in now, or should we push it out a bit?"

"Out just a bit." It was twenty feet from the waterline. Yeah, it needed to go out a bit.

Katie undid the rope, and grabbing the boat's stern, she dragged it down and dropped the back end into the water. Holding the line, she called to her friend to jump in. Within two minutes, they were transferring Winnie's bag to the Dude.

"Is that seal still here?" Winnie had the two boats gunwale to gunwale, as if the previous day's seal might find even an inch an open invitation that it couldn't refuse.

"I have an oar. I'll beat it into submission if it shows up." Katie held one up, but she smiled.

"I'm not teasing." Winnie began to sing very softly as she climbed over, "Rock-a-bye baby . . ."

Katie took a deep breath. Maybe this was not a good idea. Even so, once they were settled inside the

Dude, Winnie looked around, got out a scarf, and tied her hair into a bundle at the crown of her head. As Katie readied the boat to leave, her friend became very animated, even asking about how the boat moved without a motor.

"How much do you want to know?" Katie was pleased at her friend's change in attitude, and she leaned forward to untie from the mooring.

"Talk to me like I don't know anything." Winnie took the line from her while she stood to release the sail, and she dropped it on the floor.

"Easy enough, because I suspect it's true. Okay, mast." She patted the tall pole the sail attached to. "That was the painter I just handed you, and you just dropped the painter on the keel. That's the low spot that runs up and down the length of the boat."

"Oh, oh. I'm following you, Sweetie! Mast, keel, painter. I think I might even get this. Why painter? It looks like a rope to me." Winnie smiled, very bright eyed and interested looking.

"So you don't tie up the boat with this one. It's the mainsheet." She held up the one attached to the corner of the sail. "Or this one. It's the reef line." She pulled at a series of small cords attached to the center of the sail.

"I get that one. In case we hit a reef, we tie up with those." Winnie grinned.

"Not exactly, but you're getting closer. Each one gets a different name so we know which one we want to use." Katie had the sail untied, and she handed the loose end to Winnie. "That's the clew of the sail, but that's probably TMI. I'll say back, top and front."

"Good. I know those terms." Winnie pulled on the sail, only to have it catch the wind and tip the boat sideways.

"Whoa. Keep it loose until I'm seated." Katie dropped beside her friend. "Now grab this line and feed it through here." She touched a metal eye with a pulley attached.

"The mainsheet, right?" Winnie held it up and smiled. "See, I do listen."

"Yes, you do. Feed it through, and I'll let you control the sail. I'll operate the rudder."

"That thingie?" She pointed to the wooden stick at the back of the boat.

"Yep. When you're ready, pull that rope just until you feel the boat start to move forward. Not too tight."

The boat started to glide forward, the sail tightening; and the water slipped by under them. It made a low-pitched whooshing sound as it disappeared out of sight.

"We're sailing!" Winnie hooted. "Me! I'm sailing!"

"You are. Very good, Honey." Katie turned the rudder just a bit to keep the sail trimmed. "You want to go faster? Pull the mainsheet a little tighter, a tiny bit at a time. Let it off if you want to slow down."

She aimed for the inside route that ran between Settler's Island and Rockhaven. That would avoid most of the wind, and hopefully it would die down by the time they returned. Not too much, because then they couldn't return at all, but enough not to kill Winnie's fun.

As they passed the Point, and Carver Cove drifted by on their port side, she pointed the dock out to Winnie, telling her it was hers, and they could walk over and dive off it if they wanted. At the De Groot's, she pointed to the old house as it revealed itself, giving a little history. She steered expertly around ledges that had exposed themselves with the falling tide by paying attention to the masses of seaweed billowing just under the surface of the water.

By the time they reached town, Winnie had given up control of the sail, and she sat to one side trailing her hand in the water. It seemed the dangers of the marauding seal were forgotten, and Rockhaven Island might have finally captured her friend's heart.

"Is this how we get to church on Sunday?" Winnie had her phone out snapping pictures of the shorefront houses lining both sides of the harbor. A ferry was docked, and cars were moving off and onto the island.

"It's a twelve-mile walk if you want to come the other way. But sure, this is how I'm planning on coming."

"In our dress clothes?"

Katie found that amusing. "No, we bring our things in a waterproof bag, and then change before church."

"You're teasing." Winnie turned her phone and snapped a photo of Katie holding the rudder. "What about our hair?"

"You comb it out. Get parked. We're coming to the float, and I have to drop the sail and dock without killing you, me, or anyone else's boat. Head low!" She snapped the sail to the opposite side of the boat, held the rudder with her foot for a minute, and began to gather up the sail as she walked forward. Wrapping the mainsheet around the mast, she snapped up the painter and stepped off the bow onto the float just as the Lil' Dude came to a rest.

"That was good. You know your stuff, Sweetie!" Winnie clapped several times.

"I grew up doing this. It was learn or be stranded on the Point for three months at a time. Let me help you off." She already had the boat tied up, and she held the stern against the float for Winnie to climb out.

"Katie? Katie Carver?"

Katie looked up to see a plump, round-faced woman with a baseball cap and light brown hair walking across the parking lot above. She went blank for a moment, trying to place the face, when a boy about nine ran up and threw his arms around her.

"Make Kevie stop, Mom!"

A bigger boy, maybe two years older and looking very much like the woman, ran up and grabbed his arm and yanked him loose.

"You weasel. You didn't either see me kick that dog. Come back here." He pulled the smaller boy by the collar and dragged him away, with the first boy stumbling to keep up.

With that, Katie knew who this was. She had been thin as a kid, but with those boys, it could be only one person.

"Janine Roscoe? How have you been?" Katie waved.

"Not Roscoe in a long time. I'm Peavey now. Those were two of my boys. It's good to see you back. Are you still a Carver?"

"That's me, always a Carver. How've you been?" From Jeff's description, she had a pretty good idea, but it was polite to ask.

"Too many kids. Too many winters cooped up inside, but other than that? It's a life. You. You look good. You haven't shown your face here since the day your gramma's place out there burned. Are you rebuilding?"

Janine waited for them, talking down from the lip of the ramp. As Katie and Winnie reached the top, it was clear that Janine, short when they were kids, had already reached her full height even then.

Katie laughed. "Not this summer. Janine, this is my good friend Winnie from Boston. Winnie, meet Janine Peavey."

"Pleased to meet you." Winnie took her hand and pumped it several times. "You live here on the island, right?" She glanced at Katie for confirmation.

"Katie told you about me?" Janine seemed very pleased. "I was born on the mainland, but I've been here since I was three months. When I got married, I knew I was here forever." She laughed as if it wasn't what she'd intended, but rather what had happened. "Is this your first time out?"

"Yes. I left my car back on land, and I came out on the boat. Now we're using that little boat down there." Winnie pointed to the Dude tied up to the town float.

"The Lil' Dude. Jeff took it out for you." Janine

laughed. "I kept telling him he should use it, but no, he had it in his boat house, working on it every summer. He said you'd be back some day, and now he's proved right. I remember us out in that little boat a few times."

"More than a few." Katie laughed along with Janine, hearing in the woman's words what she wasn't saying. *He said you'd be back.* And he worked on it every summer?

"Surely you brought your car out." It was Janine again, talking to Katie. "Did you make it down the drive all right?"

"It hasn't been cleared. It's the Lil' Dude or nothing for us, I'm afraid. Jeff took me to the Point, but we're afoot the rest of our stay."

"Oh, no. You could've made it down fine. I was out there in my car just last week. I'm the one who cleaned the cabin for you." A boy down the street darted from behind a building and yelled, and Janine said, "I'm sorry. Those boys! I've got to go. Maybe we can get together before you head off island again. Bye. You, too, Winnie!"

She turned and ran toward the screaming boy.

"Driveway?" Winnie put her hands on her hips. "We have a driveway, and I left my car there?" She pointed with her hand out the harbor the direction they'd sailed in.

"Actually, it's that way." Katie pulled her friend's arm around to point towards town. "Over the island and past Carver Point. But yes, you left your car there."

"Can I go get it?" Winnie huffed. "If I can drive, I

want my car."

"You can, if you want to pay nearly a hundred dollars to bring it over."

"How much?" Winnie's eyes went wide.

"But you don't need to." This, Katie found amusing.

"Why not? I do need a car, so I can get to church Sunday, to church without changing clothes when I get to the door." She said that with emphasis.

"Why not?" Katie took her friend's chin and pointed her face towards the other end of the parking lot. "Because that's my car there."

"Oh! Beetle, Beetle, I love you, in red, white or the color blue!" Winnie clapped excitedly. A bright blue Volkswagen Beetle sat in the very last space.

"There is one issue, though."

"Not if we have a car." Winnie threw her arms around her friend and gave her cheek a quick peck. "We've got a car!"

"But the keys are at the cabin."

The dismay on Winnie's face was truly hilarious, and as hard as she tried, Katie could not keep from laughing. Even when Winnie slapped her on the arm and told her it wasn't funny at all, she continued to laugh until tears ran down her face.

11

"**J**effrey Ragsdale!" Intentionally, very intentionally, Katie walked up behind the man she was trying so hard to avoid, and she poked him on the shoulder.

"Katie!" A smile broke out on his face as he turned to her.

"Don't you smile at me. I just talked to Janine Roscoe. Peavey. I just talked to Janine Peavey, and you didn't want me to talk to her, did you? Four kids? Nah. I met two of them, and they were perfectly nice. You didn't want me to know she'd been out there at my cabin. Well, she told me. What do you think of that?"

Katie stepped back just enough that they weren't touching, but she refused to retreat. The pecking order was out of kilter here, and Jeff needed to be set straight. She might not have been around the past four-teen years, but she wouldn't be lied to the moment she returned. She would not!

"They are hellions, Katie. I didn't lie about that." He turned to the older man he'd been sharing a plate of food with, and he explained. "The Peavey boys."

"Ah. Janine and Al's brood." He nodded with a smile, as if that explained it all. "They do have energy to spare."

"Why didn't you tell me the drive was cleared? Winnie and I have been sailing back and forth in the Dude, and I have a car here on island." That had her irritated as much as anything. She'd endured that ride out in his boat. Now, Winnie. Was he trying to make her life difficult?

"You used to enjoy the Dude." He didn't seem per-turbed. "I thought you'd enjoy having her out there to use."

"I do, and thank you, but that's not the point. I have my car here, and you didn't tell me the drive is cleared."

"You didn't ask." The man with him chuckled, and Jeff held his hand up to quiet him. "Not now, Roker."

"Okay, but you brought this on yourself, if you ask me."

"Jeff! What about my drive?" She had left Winnie at the Paper Store looking at magazines, because she didn't think she needed to see her take on Jeff Rags-dale, but she was about to get angry.

"I told you I'd kept up a presence at the place." He had one arm on the back of the chair by then, and he was sitting sideways in his seat. "Would you like some shrimp? It's from Harbor View."

Roker pulled his hand away. He'd almost emptied the plate.

"When I called Marc—"

"When you called Marc, you told him you needed a boat out to Carver Point, and would he set something up. He set me up. Were you unhappy with the service? I'll be glad to offer you a full refund on my services."

"I didn't pay you anything." With her words, the amount she owed blossomed into the ride out, the work he'd done on the Dude, the Point, for Janine's cleaning. All of it.

"Okay, so if you didn't pay me, and you're dissatisfied, then I can only give you a refund by paying you. All my money's wrapped up in lobster, so I guess that means we have to have that lobster bake out at your place. I've got it penciled in for tomorrow about seven. Are we still good with that?"

"I—" She had worked herself into a corner, but she wasn't sure it was one of her own making.

"Careful, Jeff." That was Roker, and his amusement came through just fine.

From down the street, Winnie called, "There you are. Oh, hi, Jeffie! Are we still doing our cookout?"

"Are we, Katie?" He still had his arm over the back of the chair, and he was fighting a smile. From the other direction she caught the sound of Janine chewing on one of her boys.

"Stop it, Konnar. That's my friend down there from when I grew up, and I refuse to let her see you

88

like this." He kicked her and ran off down the street.

"Will you bring Janine? No kids?" Then it would be like a gift to her old friend, a gift of a few hours without her trying children. It wouldn't be a date in any form or fashion.

"Janine? Al won't be happy babysitting." That was Roker again. By now, the plate was completely empty.

"For you, done." Jeff held a hand out to shake.

"No you don't, Jeff Ragsdale. Right now I don't trust you to the end of this street. I'm not shaking any hand you hold out to me."

"Smart girl." Roker chuckled.

"Jeffie! How sweet!" Winnie appeared at Katie's side, and she took Jeff's extended hand in both of hers. She massaged it for a moment, her eyes going wide. "Sweetie, you need to feel this man's hand. It's all muscle, like a real man's hand."

"Oh, you two are made for each other!" Katie turned and walked away. She crossed the street and stopped at the edge of the lot overlooking the harbor. It seemed she'd developed an ongoing exit strategy. Blow up, cross the street, and stop at the ramp down to the town float. She couldn't even be creative, maybe go in the Paper Store and slam the door, or get in her car and speed away.

Now, she'd invited him to her beach for an entire evening. If she'd just stayed away, then everything would've been fine. She wouldn't have seen him again, and . . . and . . .

That wasn't what she wanted at all. She wanted what she'd seen in that picture from over a dozen years ago. She wanted fourteen, and to be in a dinghy on the mud flats with all her friends, and to be looking into the eyes of a boy who'd just dug up a giant clam in hopes of making a boatload of money.

The other thing she remembered, their venture had gone south in a heartbeat. No one had wanted to buy their clams, they'd begun to stink in their tub, and they'd had to throw them all into the harbor. For a week after that, no one had come to the Point, and she'd felt useless and abandoned.

It was that same feeling now. Her trip to Rockhaven was heading south in a heartbeat. All the people she knew, all the places that had been so familiar to her weren't quite the same as they had been.

She wasn't the same as she had been.

She was stronger. She had her place in Boston, she worked with people she liked, and Winnie was her best friend. She could hang on to that, couldn't she?

The float below caught her eye. She still had to sail back to the Point, and the tide didn't turn for another four hours. How could she stay in town with Jeff Ragsdale right behind her for another four hours?

The ferry horn blew, and across the harbor, its diesel engines began to roar. The massive ship with its half-empty deck pushed the water aside to the complaints of a dozen or so birds. Several people, probably daytrippers, had gone up top already, and one figure had a camera out. He paused, shifted position, paused, and shifted again. He was memorizing Rockhaven. To him, when he looked at his pictures, it would always be exactly the way it looked today.

What about her pictures? In her pictures, Rockhaven was a big white house, friends she couldn't wait to return to every summer, and a life that was more of a dream than the best dream possible.

Where had those pictures gone?

Her only answer was the sound of Winnie's voice, loud and laughing, and Jeff's deep-throated laughter in return. Those weren't the memories in her pictures, and she didn't have any way to change the pages in her photo album and make them new.

She didn't even have the help of God, not really. He had left her to go her own way a long time ago.

Five more days. She could do this five more days, and then she'd be gone. She was that strong, strong enough to do this five more days. And Winnie? That girl had better be her right hand man. After all, she was sleeping in the bed next to hers. They were a team, and not even Jeff Ragsdale was going to break them apart.

She took a deep breath, turned and began her walk across the parking lot, determined this time to be the strong woman she knew she had become.

If Jeff didn't like it? Tough. That was just the way it was.

12

The sky had hunkered down, and heavy rain threatened. The wind spiked the water with jerky little hats of white foam, and anyone normal would avoid open water.

That was fine with Katie. It matched her mood. It did something else, also. It had convinced her soon-to-be-ex-friend to hitch a ride with her new Jeffie-friend to the cabin.

It also kept either of them from seeing the tears she refused to wipe from her face.

She had been mortified to find herself greeted by Jeff Ragsdale when she had arrived on the island, and she had rebuffed him at every opportunity. Then she had lashed out at him in town, making her position as clear as pie on his face.

Nothing had fazed the man. Nothing. It was like

that boy from the picture. It didn't matter how much mud he had to dig through, or what was in the mud that was splattered all over him; when he had a goal in mind, the goal was the only thing he saw.

What did he expect from her? She wasn't an island girl, no matter how strongly she'd wished for that very thing all those years ago. Her time away had been just long enough that she'd seen the way the world really was. It was a high-rise apartment, a cubicle in an insurance company's claim division, and regular car payments every month. Islands were for summer vacations and the occasional free weekend. Life on an island? That was for Janine trapped during the brutal months of winter with four wild animals. It was probably the reason they were wild in the first place. Winter and too many hours of darkness could do that to a person.

Now Katie flew from the harbor. The Lil' Dude did what she did best: She surfed along the tops of the waves, the centerboard holding her true, and the tiller vibrating against Katie's hand. She had reefed the sail, and still, the wind was a fist that drove the Dude forward.

It was glorious, it was hard, and it was just what she needed to bleed out her anger and frustration. She wrapped the mainsheet around her hand, and she pulled it taut, the tell-tales straight out and perpendicular to the mast. Occasionally the bow slammed into a swell, and a fine mist wet Katie's clothes. It also wet her face, filling her eyes with moisture.

Of course she admitted nothing otherwise, that the

moisture might have been there even without the ocean spray. It was the salt that made her eyes burn, because salt water did that, didn't it? She had to watch for re-membered underwater ledges, to dart between sea-weed-covered outcroppings, and to pull up sailing skills from a childhood that had been snatched from an innocent girl just when her life was truly taking form. How could she worry about damp eyes at a time like this?

She was halfway to the Point before she realized the water hitting her face was there whether the Dude was flinging spray through the air or not. Slipping into the passage between Settler's and the island only made her mast lines buzz with intensity, and the little Dude became a frisky mare, filled with fight, and ready to spar with her jockey.

Katie sparred back, giving the controls the one-two. The sail was already reefed, but she had a few remembered skills up her sleeve. She tucked the boat next to Settler's, with the mast barely clearing the low-hanging spruce that would brush the water at highest tide, and just before the little boat crossed in front of the massive De Groot dock, she gave the tiller a hard push and skimmed around Little Goose Ledge, skirting the hidden rocks and their seaweed icing before they slammed into the bottom of the boat. For years, she remembered the tales of those who had holed their craft on Little Goose, but never Katie. She prided her-self in that.

It was going across the mouth of the Cove that could be dangerous. The tidal bore was in full throttle by now, and it could easily pull a craft as small as the Dude right inside. That was what she would have normally done as a girl in weather like this, dart in through the tumbled fists of massive stones that gripped Carver Cove in its embrace, and landed her craft, cowering against the elements under the safety of the sturdy granite pillars that were the entrance to her grandmother's oceanfront home.

No, not today. That home had been taken from her. The cabin was hers now, all that was left from a life that had been ripped from her, and she would master the voyage to the life she now lived. The wind might beat at her, and the waves might pummel her craft, but she was master of the seas, and none could best her skills.

She was adrenalin charged and so pumped up by the time she saw the little plastic boat that her victorious conquest was all that mattered to her. It was when she released the sail to grab the mooring that she realized a storm had truly overtaken the sky. The rain was steady, and it bit into her skin with icy pricks that could only come in a northern summer gale.

"This might get bad," she muttered, loop-loop-and-tucking the line. If so, she had one more job to do. She reached under the seat and pulled out an oiled, waterproof canvas sheet. After Janine's comments in town, she had known it would be here. Jeff would have made sure of it. Along the outside edges, rope was strung through grommets. She expected it would slip over the top of the cockpit perfectly, and the lines would mate up precisely with the cleats around the boat. Keeping water out meant keeping the boat afloat in weather like this.

Securing the sail, she shook out the canvas cover and began at one corner. Looping the rope, one cleat at a time, she was pleased to make quick progress. The rain was getting heavier, and her adrenalin-infused enthusiasm was wearing thin. She wanted to get in.

She was now chilled, too.

Finally reaching the shore, she dragged the plastic skiff into the trees, turning it upside down and tying it tightly. No good losing a good boat, and she didn't intend to swim out to the Dude, not in this weather.

She ran toward the cabin, her feet slipping on the wet stones. Once she nearly went down, and she laughed at her own clumsiness. The lights were on, and that made her happy. When she started from town, she hadn't wanted to see Winnie when she arrived. She had wanted to be alone. Now? She would appreciate the company.

The door opened as she jumped up on the deck, and Katie laughed and waved at the familiar head of strawberry hair.

"Winnie! Am I glad to see you!"

"Hurry, Sweetie. I'm getting all wet. We worried you might not make it." Winnie gabbed Katie's elbow as she darted through the door, brushing water from her face.

"We?" Katie patted her friend on the cheek. "You, maybe. I didn't doubt myself for a minute."

"Me, mostly." The deep voice was resonant, complementing the pattering rain on the roof. There at the desk sat the very nemesis that had driven Katie to the sea in the first place.

"Jeff." Katie brushed her face again with her hands, then pulled her hair back to squeeze out what water she could. "Did you bring the lobster out? I don't think they'll fit in the fridge." She smiled and shrugged.

He rolled his eyes and stood, looking out into the fading light. He was still for a short time, his shoulders broad under his heavy shirt, and his hair a wild tuft of dark, shining moss careening from a stolid mound of ancient stone. Then, he shifted, and he was alive once again, as he turned to face her.

"Is that the only reason you think I came out?" His mouth seemed to want to smile, as if he found his question amusing, but there was redness in his eyes. He glanced at Winnie, then back to her, but he didn't say anything else, as if it was her turn to talk.

"Maybe?" Katie looked to Winnie to see if she was any help, only to see her friend shrug. She tried again. "To bring Winnie back in warm, dry comfort, maybe?" She looked back to Jeff.

He pressed his lips tight, and he looked away with a sour chuckle.

"What's that for?" Katie knew she'd missed something. It was warmer inside, but not much, and she shivered.

"A decade and a half, and you're the same as you were back then." He glanced at her. "I should have expected it, but I guess I made you into what I wanted, and that's my fault."

"And that means?" She was serious. How was she the same? She had been a happy-go-lucky girl then, one that was willing to fall in love when it landed on her doorstep each June, and willing to wait for its return when she left each fall. She wasn't that girl anymore. She was strong and independent, and she would tell anyone who asked her so.

He looked at her and shook his head. He stepped to Winnie and took her hand, then he patted it and said, "See you tomorrow. It'll be fun." He turned to Katie. "The weather's just a squall that'll blow over by morning, so your car won't be a problem. Full sun the rest of the day. I'd like to come out early and set up if you don't mind. I've invited a few people you might remember. I want you to have fun. You'll try?"

He grabbed her hand as he stepped by, releasing it as he moved into the blustery rain. The screen slammed, and the floor began to darken with increasing spatters of moisture. Katie closed the door.

"Okay, Winnie. What did you say to him?" Katie crossed her arms and tried to look severe, although she was pretty sure the sound of her wet clothes every time she moved didn't do much for an angry look.

"You're dripping." Winnie giggled and pointed to the floor. "Somebody's got to clean it up."

"That's not what I asked. What did you tell him?"

"Sweetie, he just gave me a ride home, that's all. Oh, we stopped by his house." Her face brightened. "It's on the water, and it has a real kitchen, and a bathroom and everything. You should try it here at your place sometime."

"And? All that was for?"

"Towels! We brought towels!" Winnie opened a large bag on her bed, and she pulled out two towels striped in cream, blue, and red. "Here! One to dry your hair, and the other to dry everything else. Jeffie is so sweet. He thinks of everything!"

"I bet he does!" Katie grabbed the closest towel, and she began to work it roughly over her hair. She couldn't help but be thankful in some small way, because she hadn't brought any at all. What really bothered her was what Jeff said.

How was she the same? After her long, uphill climb to find out just who she was, and learning to be strong in the process, how could she be the same in any way, fashion, or form?

Maybe Jeff was an idiot, and she'd never figured that out all those years ago. Yeah, that was right, the island idiot that couldn't find a rock ledge in broad daylight, and that had been God's plan all along. God had rescued her, and she hadn't even known.

She laughed at that idea, because it hadn't felt like a rescue back then. Now? She'd take any help she could get to get her out of this pickle.

"I knew it would be just fine." Winnie laughed and put her arm around Katie. "See? You're happy again. I got you a file, and I posted another picture of you." She pulled out a fingernail file from one pocket, laying it on the bed, and her phone from the other. "See?"

The post was her in the Dude just leaving the town float. One arm was back, pulling the sail taut, and the other held the tiller. A small bow wave curled up the side. Her hair was tossed by the wind, and she looked angry.

"You can unpost that, you know." Katie turned away and continued to rub her hair. She should be smiling and happy in her pictures. Then she would re-member Rockhaven as a happy time in her life. That picture? Who would find her life attractive if they looked at that?

"Oh, I don't know." Winnie sat on her folding bed, her face buried in her phone. "I might wait to see what Jeffie thinks."

"What Jeffie thinks?" Katie looked at her and snorted.

"Sure." She laid back, holding the phone in the air. "There! He came through, just like he said he would. That's the Jeffie I like so much!" She turned it for Katie to see.

"Did he tell you he loves you?" Katie was down to her arms, and she smirked at her friend.

"Well, I think he means you, so I'm not really sure."

Katie grabbed the phone and she looked under the picture. There by his name was a little yellow happy face. She held the phone back out to her friend.

"See? You make him happy." Winnie held the phone to her chest, just where her heart would be. "Happiness is so hard to find."

"Especially in a cabin in the woods." Katie began to strip her wet things off. "Sometimes good friends are hard to find, too."

"That's why I'm glad I found you." Winnie stood

with a bright look on her face. "I need to visit the potty. I'll be right back." She pulled an umbrella from behind the door.

"Where did that come from?" Katie knew she hadn't brought it.

"This? From Jeffie." She smiled, opened the door, popped the umbrella open, and disappeared down the path, the bright sound of rain on the fabric quickly fading away.

Of course. Jeffie. Katie had to admit, he was doing all the right things. He was checking every box, and Winnie was eating it up. Her? She couldn't figure him out, and that bothered her. After what he said earlier, it bothered her more than she liked to admit.

13

Everything dripped with the remains of the night's downpour, but the sky was clear. The sun would be fully up before long, but for now, Katie enjoyed her lighthouse sundial being completely shaded. It gave her something to look forward to, like she owned a part of Rockhaven that no one else knew about.

She unfolded the lounger from the day before and positioned it at the best viewing angle. Pulling her robe tight, she slipped out of her shoes and pulled her feet up and covered them. Now all she had to do was wait on the sun.

She closed her eyes for a minute to soak in the sounds of the fresh island morning: the dripping branches shedding last night's rain; the water undulating against the rocks on the shore; even the occasional ding, ding of a buoy bell. It was so peaceful she felt she could stay in this one spot forever.

"Sweetie?" The word was whispered, and the screen door bumped closed quietly with no more than a soft thump.

"Yes?" Katie didn't want the morning disturbed.

"I came to keep you company." The second lounger clicked softly as it unfolded.

"Sure. Quiet, though. I'm waiting for the lighthouse to light up. I finally made it out before the sun hit it."

"You've been up a long time." Winnie's chair creaked, telling that she had sat down.

"No, I just got out here." She had been about to open her eyes and check on its progress when her friend came out. Now she was having trouble opening them at all.

"You better hurry if you want to catch it before the sun's to the bottom. It's about to ring the magic day-time bell."

"It's what?" Katie sat up, forcing her eyes open. "Oh, Winnie! I missed it! My third morning here, and I still haven't seen it at first light."

"Shush! Shush! It's okay, Sweetie. I got it for you. It's already posted." She held out her phone.

Sure enough, shot through the screen on one of the windows were several grainy photos of the lighthouse, the first one with the sun just lighting the very top, and several more as it slipped toward the water.

"You got up to do this?" Katie looked to see if there were any likes, but they were all blank. It was early, though, so that didn't mean anything. Every other normal person was still asleep.

"Almost. My arm got up." Winnie was snuggled under her electric blanket, although it wasn't attached to a cord. Her hair was a fluffy halo of a pillow, and her eyes were closed. "I heard you, and I knew you were having a little love time with your beach, so every few minutes I held my phone up and took a picture. But me? Nah! I like nine o'clock too much to get up just for a sunrise."

"You're here now. Why the rush?"

"I was lonely, and I like your company. I thought maybe you like mine, since you invited me here. Do you? After yesterday, I wasn't real sure."

"I couldn't be here without you." Katie reached over and patted the electric blanket. When she found Winnie's arm, she squeezed it. "Who else would stay with me in a cabin with no bathroom, no running water, and no curtains?"

"We may have a little company after a bit." Winnie said the words carefully, as if she was afraid they might not be taken well.

"Not your Jeffie, please." Katie took her hand back. She hoped she hadn't lied. She laid the phone on the top of Winnie's blanket.

"We do need the car." Winnie looked at her imploringly, her eyes pleading.

"I put your phone there."

"I feel it. Is the car okay?" She smiled.

"Is it Janine?"

"Oh, she could have done it, I suppose, and I bet

she wouldn't mind. Then she could visit with you and make up for old times. That would be so sweet. I didn't even think. So sorry." Winnie had begun to smile, and her eyes were closed again.

"Okay, Cheshire Cat. Spill the beans, or I'm taking a picture of you sleeping and post it on the Internet."

"Here." She took the phone and held it out to Katie. "I look cute when I sleep."

"What makes you think that?" Katie took the phone and found the camera, held it up and snapped a picture.

"I have to be. Just look at me." She shrugged under the blanket, but her eyes remained closed. "I can't help what I am. Want me to post it?" She held out her hand.

"Oh, you. Sure. You post it." She slapped the phone into the open hand. "It is Jeff, isn't it? You can have him, you know."

"He's not my Jeffie. He's your Jeffie. I asked him for a ride to pick up your car last night, and he said it had to be early. He has to take the ferry to town."

"He does, does he? I guess I need to get dressed. First ferry's at seven."

"Thank you, Sweetie. I think I'll go back to bed now."

"I thought you were here to keep me company."

"Only until you said yes. You've done that now." She stood with her blanket wadded in her hands. "I might leave the lounger, if it's okay with you."

A horn caught their attention. Katie sat up. "He's here, already?"

"Be kind, Sweetie. I told him you said for me to

105

ask. That's probably why he was so confused last night. Sorry. I didn't get a chance to tell you." Winnie scuttled inside the door and was gone.

So that was what he meant by "her car wouldn't be a problem."

"Katie? I can't take long. I'll miss the ferry." The words echoed in the quiet, carrying over the Point.

She guessed there was no time to change. She stepped inside and grabbed her purse, and then she headed up the path, pink housecoat and all. The ferry didn't wait. That she knew. If she wasn't there when Jeff needed to go, he would drive off without her. He had no choice.

She was curious about why he was headed to the mainland. He'd been insistent about the lobster bake being at seven, but anyplace off island was an all-day venture. One way was nearly an hour and a half, and that didn't count the wait time in line before the ferry loaded. Without a reservation, two hours was the minimum for getting there early. The spots were first come, first served.

As she topped the rise, she passed by the old foundation of her grandmother's burned-out house. She cringed and refused to look, more than just a glance. The stone still rose above the ground several feet on one end, and nearly a full story on the other. Left through a gate were the parking area and the drive. Just past it would be Jeff, waiting to hustle her to her car.

The gate, an old wooden one, was the first item she'd seen on the Point that was in poor repair. It was cocked open, and the paint was peeling. It looked like the main post had rotted completely through at the base.

Past it was a shiny green Jeep with fat tires and a fabric roof. That made her smile. Who on the island would waste money on such a frivolous car? A truck, or an SUV, perhaps, because off-road capabilities were in demand during the long winter months, but even she found the Jeep a bit showy.

Jeff had his door open, and he stood on the sill looking over the roof. "Good morning, Katie. I know it's early, but I didn't know it was that early."

"I expected you later." She waved. Like five o'clock in the afternoon, but she didn't say that. There was no point. He was here, the ferry was leaving, and to get her car, this was the only logical way.

"Hey, I don't care. I'm just glad you asked for my help. I'm glad to do it. Climb in." He dropped into his seat and shut his door.

"I bet you are," she muttered. Here she was again. She had started out the week in his boat, bumped into him every time she went out, and now she was riding in his car. If she wasn't careful, people who saw her would think she'd gone totally native.

However, Janine Roscoe Peavey was not what she wanted to become. Four marauding kids and a look on her face that said "What have I got myself into" didn't cut it for the city girl Katie'd become. Coming back was on her own terms, and this place had better plan to deal with it.

She slammed the door when she got in, and she

glared at Jeff.

"Okay," he said. "Fine by me. I won't say a word." He shifted the Jeep into reverse, and in a few moments, they were headed down the drive, the big tires and soft suspension swaying a whole lot more than was exactly comfortable for anyone just out of bed.

Katie hoped she didn't lose her stomach, and she was very glad she hadn't had anything to eat. And Winnie thought being on the water was bad. For a second time, she glared at Jeff, but she found he refused to look her way.

She couldn't get satisfaction even from that. This was not going to be a fun day.

"You remember your keys?" Jeff said the words very softly.

Katie grabbed her purse from the floor and dropped it on the console. "Yes, I have my keys."

"Okay. My mouth is closed." He ran a finger over his lips, zipping them up, but he had a smile underneath.

"Oh," she growled, looking away. What really irked her was that he'd gotten better looking in the years she'd been away. How did that happen, and why to her? He should be fat and bald, and then she wouldn't care.

She couldn't wait to get to her car. It wasn't safe for her being cooped up with Jeff Ragsdale, not safe at all.

14

Katie listened to the sounds of the Jeep as Jeff down-shifted one gear at a time to slow for town. Once they were past the potholes and granite rock heaves that made up much of the driveway, he had pushed the off-road vehicle to nearly sixty. It was heart stopping on the island's narrow roads.

"Ferry's not loading yet." She noted the line of cars, two very small ones, and a truck filled with blocks of granite.

"It wouldn't be." He tapped the clock on the dash then pressed in the clutch and pulled the shifter into a lower gear. The engine growled its complaints.

"Thank you for doing this." She had her purse back in her lap, now uncomfortably aware of her pink house robe. Out on the Point, she'd pictured slipping from one vehicle to another and driving back to the cabin totally unnoticed. She was irritated at herself for not remembering how early island life started. Lobstermen didn't wait on eight o'clock to start up their boats. They ran by the great time clock in the sky. Daylight was their alarm, and they were in full force on the docks.

They seemed to know Jeff's car, too, calling and waving. One or two whistled, and as low as she ducked in her seat, she knew she couldn't disappear altogether.

"All you had to do was ask. Thank you for asking, by the way." He flipped the blinker on to turn in the town lot. With a slight rev of the engine, he coaxed the big tires over the low curb. The puddles from the night's rain splashed as he gained speed across the tarmac before stopping just in front of her car.

"How do you know this one's mine?"

"That's a silly question. Who else has Mass plates around here?" He turned the key off and shifted in his seat to look at her. "You know, I'm twenty-nine, and this is the first time I've ridden in a car with you."

"Your boat doesn't count, huh?" His remark was just what she'd been thinking. How many times had he driven these familiar roads, either alone or with a girl-friend, and she'd been attending high school, later college, and now working for half-a-dozen years for the insurance firm?

"Ah, my boat always counts." He leaned forward and wrapped both arms across the steering wheel, resting the side of his face on them and looking at her. "You've enjoyed the Dude, though?"

She looked at him, so boyish. She could see the fifteen-year-old from her last summer looking out of
those eyes. She laughed and looked away.

"What?"

"You. You haven't changed at all." Her eyes
burned, and they shouldn't. All connections with this
man had been scoured away years ago. It was just a
memory she'd seen in those eyes and nothing more.

"Then what has?"

She looked back at him. There on his cheek, just
where his face dimpled when he smiled, was a crease.
It was small, but it told her he smiled a lot. "Everything. Did you notice the big hole where my grandmother's house stood? That one's pretty obvious."

"Nah, the house doesn't mean anything, unless you
let it." He leaned back, keeping one arm still on the
steering wheel, and his back against the door.

"How can you say that? It changed my life."

"Stuff doesn't change your life. Not the real
changes that are important." He looked out the back of
the car the direction of the ferry landing. It was too far
to see from the town lot, but something caught his attention. "I remember the girl who rang the bell every
time I rowed up to her float." He smiled and shifted his
eyes to look at her.

"You told me already."

"Right. I did. That first day." He laughed and
looked away. "I guess I'd better get to the landing.
They'll be loading up in a minute."

"I'm glad you haven't changed." The words
slipped out before Katie could cut them off. She put

111

her hand on the console, an ordinary gesture for an ordinary situation, but one she was aware of as very risky in this situation.

"Oh, I doubt that's true." He looked at her hand for a moment, then with a deep breath, he turned his head to look through the windshield. "Tonight, then?" He readjusted his position and started the engine, working the gearshift into neutral. With his left leg, he let out the clutch. The engine idled noisily.

"Early, you said. Still?" Katie found she didn't want to get out. This was a small taste of what she'd enjoyed so much with Jeff all those years ago: half saying things and knowing you didn't have to say the rest; the easy pauses; and the way he moved, comfortable in himself and with the world around him. He'd been a natural on a boat; and the cornerstone of the gang. Then he'd become a hole in her life she'd never been able to fill. For this one moment, she felt some of it back. It wasn't an opened floodgate, by any means, but the trickle was nice.

He looked at her and winked. "You better go. Town's coming alive, and that's a really pink bathrobe there. Don't want anyone talking."

"Oh! I didn't even think." She was now, though. Jeff, delivering her to her car at the crack of dawn, and wearing this? Could it look any worse?

"Just go. I'll be on time." He was smiling by then.

"Let me get my keys." She dug in her purse, finally coming up with a bright yellow sunflower attached to a ring. "Don't you move until I get in that car." She looked at him hard.

"Yes, ma'am." He nodded. He did wait, but only just. Then his tires spun on the wet asphalt, and he was gone.

It didn't do much good for him to stick around, because just in front of her was Marc from the Paper Store. He waved with a smile and gave her a thumbs-up on a raised hand.

Oh, she was going to die. She was absolutely going to die!

Mortified, she started the car, working out the best way out of town to avoid being seen. Turn right, and that took her by the school. It also took her by the soccer fields and the high school track. She expected they were in use even this early: summer soccer games; joggers taking July seriously. Left were the docks and the ferry landing. Either way she was sure to be seen. Her car color didn't help. The bright blue stood out like a sore thumb.

She gritted her teeth and shifted into drive. One direction was as bad as the other, and she turned on her left blinker. It was at least shorter.

Before she got past the docks and the ferry horn sounded, more than one arm had waved to her. As she passed the landing, she felt relief no one was arriving this early. Word would be all over town. Only one man was walking the side of the road facing away from her, and he didn't look up.

Rounding the corner, she could see the ferry exiting the harbor with a whitewater tail trailing after it across the surface of the ocean. It had filled up after all, including two large trucks. At the very back of the deck was a green Jeep with a black fabric roof. Its brake lights flashed once, as if someone had shifted position inside and brushed a foot against the pedal, then immediately moved away.

It was just a glimpse. No more. Yet, as her car moved on down the road, Katie felt an empty sadness surround her. Like she'd had something, and now it was gone. Taken. Slipped through her fingers. Carried away by the ferry into lands unknown, with no news of just when it would return.

She knew what it was. It was fourteen years erased with the brush of a man's smile. It was fourteen years she wished she could live over again.

One more chance, God. Why did you take my life from me?

He hadn't. Not really. She had admitted that years before. The real problem, the real reason she couldn't forgive God was that He hadn't done anything at all. He had left her alone to learn to swim on her own, and she'd nearly drowned.

She wasn't jumping into the water again. One lobster bake and one ride to pick up her car didn't make a life preserver. If she was going to survive, she had to lock up her past tightly and keep it right where it belonged.

Sorry, Jeff, she determined. Bring lots of people, because you're going to need someone to talk to.

Her determination didn't stop the tears, though. She knew what she was giving up. However, safe was better than sorry, and when she got back to Boston, she'd be glad she'd been strong.

She just didn't feel glad now, and she didn't bother to wipe away the tears.

15

"**Y**ou cannot expect me to do this." Katie held up the two strings Winnie had handed her, and she made a face. "I tie my shoes with bigger cords than this."

They weren't exactly strings, but Katie didn't consider them much more. The fabric amounted to little more than patches compared to what she usually wore.

"Okay." Winnie didn't sound offended. "Those were just freebies from a Macy's shoot. Toss them if you want. What about this?"

She pulled out a one-piece still on a hanger that was half black and brightly flowered over the rest. An extra strap was attached to the hanger. "I'm just not sure how we'll tighten it up to stay on you. The stringy thing is easier to adjust."

"Here's our solution." Katie lifted the strap from

the inside to show it was a belt.

"Oh, you are so smart. Of course!" Winnie giggled. "Go put this on. You think soap will be okay in the water? I don't want to *pollute* or anything."

"The fish will live." Katie had jumped in, soaped up, and rinsed off by diving back in more than one time in her life. It had never done any damage that she was aware of.

She was glad Winnie had suggested this on her own. It was a sorely-needed distraction after the drive back in the car. She had been in control by the time she'd walked to the cabin, but the day seemed to stretch emptily ahead; and even the brilliant sunshine hadn't seemed to repair the pain.

Swimming off the float would be just the thing.

"Sweetie, look at this." Winnie stood at the window looking out towards the Dude. "We have water right here."

Katie had explained it once. At the float, they could leap in. Here? To get deep enough to swim meant wading in. What she didn't say was why jumping was better, but Winnie would learn. She might not be happy afterwards, but she would learn.

"See? The water's going away." Katie pointed to the exposed stones that still shimmered with water. The tide had started to turn, although it was still high. Yet, it had dropped past the edge of the deck, and it would be out several hundred feet before it finished.

"Still, we have to hike all the way over there?" Winnie already had on a two-piece, one that was conservative compared to the two strings from earlier. She held one of the striped towels under one arm.

Katie gave in a little, giving the bad news to her friend as gently as possible. "Water temperature. The sun warms the Cove, but open water is too deep, even on a day like today. Swimming off the float can mean a twenty-degree difference." It didn't mean it would be warm, but twenty degrees could mean the difference between invigorating playtime and hypothermia.

"That's a lot, I guess. Are there stickers?" Winnie wasn't wearing shoes, and the walk over the Point covered a lot of grass.

"Probably. What do you have?" Besides the blue spikes, Katie meant. Her shoes were more sensible, but she only had the one pair plus her house shoes.

"These?" Winnie pulled out a thin-soled pair of sandals, with jeweled beads for straps.

"Perfect. Just stay out of the tall grass."

"Are there snakes?" Winnie's eyes went wide.

"No. Just killer seals. They sleep in the grass." It was a mean thing to say, but Katie's emotions had been stripped bare, and she couldn't help herself.

"Now I know you're teasing." Winnie grabbed Katie's arm and laughed. "You take such good care of me, how can anything go wrong?" She gave Katie a soft peck on the cheek and walked out on the deck, humming to herself.

Katie ran through the list of things that could go wrong. They could slip and fall on the way down to the dock. The water might not be as warm as she hoped. Then there were sea urchins, the prickly kind that bloomed infections across the bottoms of your feet. There were all sorts of things that could go plenty wrong, like hearts stripped bare, old flames that had flamed out, and heavenly Fathers who hadn't acted very fatherly.

Oh, no, Winnie, she wanted to say. I can't take very good care of you at all.

Instead, she slipped on the suit, found it fit rather better than her friend had suggested, and cinched the belt up around the waist anyway. She had packed a bar of soap in her bag, and she dug until she found it. For a wash cloth, she pulled out a clean sock to drop the soap in. With the second towel in tow, she exited the cabin to join her friend.

"Ready?" She nudged Winnie who lay supine on one of the loungers.

"Sweetie, I was thinking. You know, you said that about the water temperature. Did I see a motel in town?"

"No, no. We are not renting a motel room just to take a shower." Katie pulled Winnie up from the chair. "This is the real Maine experience, and you get to live it all."

"How cold will it be?" Winnie had found sunglasses from somewhere, and she slipped them on her face. "Very much colder than Key West? I was swimming in the ocean there once."

"Oh, Honey. Maybe a degree or two. But, hey! We have sunshine and soap." Katie held up her sock and soap combination. "What else do we need?" Besides hot water, she thought, but the less warning given about that the better.

"And towels, from Jeffie's." Winnie held hers up and smiled.

"Sure. And Jeffie's towels. Now, about tonight, the tide won't be all the way out when everyone arrives, but by the time we set up the cookout, we'll have quite a bit of room on the rocks. It's safer with the fire that way." Katie talked as they headed across the Point. The trail would lead right past Carver House's empty grave, and the turn in the conversation was to get them to the other side. She needed time to get used to the hole. She should have considered that her friend's inquisitive nature would lead her right to it.

"Your grandmother's house was big." Winnie stopped the conversation in full swing. "What are these steps going down?"

"They led to the basement." It would be easier if they walked on by, and Katie made a try to move her friend along. "It's probably filled with raccoons and mice now."

"Ooh! They won't get me if I look over, will they?" She walked through overgrown grass to peer into the sunken cavern. "I thought there would be boards and stuff inside. Where's everything that didn't get burned?"

"Everything got burned." Her parents had received the bill for clearing away the debris, from a local man suggested by the town council and hired for the job. With the disaster that had happened, and six months later to have to pay for cleaning up everything that was left? That had been the final straw for them, and the property had sat unloved and unused for all the intervening years.

"Janine said you could build a new house on top of this." Winnie smiled brightly, as if that resolved the whole issue.

"Maybe, if an engineering survey tested it out as sound. Somebody could rebuild, anyway. I work and make a car payment, remember? I have no money."

They moved on, and just ahead the dock came into view. So did the Cove. The water sparkled in the sun, and the trees lining the shore looked unreal in their perfection. There was just enough of a breeze to put the swing on the old apple tree in motion, and it was beautiful.

"Forget that old motel in town. This is my bathtub." Winnie pushed her hair from her face when the breeze caught it. "This is *Sound of Music* beautiful."

"Or *Under a Tuscan Sun*." Katie knew how her friend felt, though. She had lived this for all of her childhood, and it had always felt that way to her.

"Me first!" Winnie took off down the path, her beaded sandals catching in the sun, her towel held high in one hand. "Come on, Katie! This will be fun!"

"I have the soap," Katie called after her. It was fun watching someone else finding so much enjoyment in this place she'd loved dearly. Walking more slowly down the path to the dock, she idly ran a finger over the nails she had filed nearly completely away. When they were still broken, she'd at least remembered how beautiful they were. Once they were filed, they didn't catch on stuff anymore, and she was able to put them out of her thoughts. They had become nothing, not a nuisance, not beautiful, nothing. But the thing was, she didn't enjoy them anymore. They would have to grow out before she could appreciate them again, and that was something she couldn't rush. She would have to file them, shape them, and it would happen a little at a time. Yet, if she was patient, she would have her fingernails back again, just as beautiful as before.

She saw the connection, one that she would have once attributed to a caring and almighty God. Her relationship with this island and with Jeff was her fingernail. It had been torn and made ugly. She had improved it, but only by slicing away everything she had loved. It no longer hurt, but only because it was no longer there.

In the process of repairing the pain, she had lost something very beautiful. The only way to get it back was to give it a chance to grow once again. If she continually filed away every entreaty Jeff made, all she would ever have would be nubs on her heart, and that wasn't very appealing at all.

The in-between stage wasn't enjoyable, though. That's the part she dreaded. Anyway, she only had four days. How much could a fingernail grow in only four days?

Lots of luck there!

Just then she heard Winnie scream, and Katie took off running down the hill.

16

Winnie's scream was a serious false alarm.

Katie found that out only after slipping once on the grass and racing to the end of the dock to look down at her friend standing on the float running her hands up and down her arms.

"What's wrong?" she called down, still catching her breath. "Are you hurt?"

"Do you know how cold the water is? I have chill bumps all up and down my legs. You should have told me." Winnie sounded particularly peeved.

"That's why I didn't." Katie patted her chest, glad to have her heart under control. She started down the ramp, seeing that there was even a ladder on the side of the float. Good. It was easier to exit the water with a ladder. Someone, meaning Jeff, had been very thorough about keeping things in good repair.

At the bottom, she dumped her things on the float, and she pulled out her sock and the bar of soap. "This early in the season, I would have suggested soaping up before you jump in. Then, if you're freezing, you don't have to take another dip." She had the soap slipped into the sock by then, and she dipped it in the water and began scrubbing her leg. She made a face. "That *is* cold."

"Yeah. It is." Winnie didn't sound very forgiving.

"You warm up while I go first. You have to do this, though." She pointed the soap at her friend then dipped it back in the water and continued working on the grass stain on her leg. "See this green spot? This is where I slipped when you screamed. Maybe I should make you go first."

"Not me. My chill bumps are still bumpy."

"Who cares about your funny little chill bumps?" Katie grinned impishly, reminded of long-ago friends on the island joining her on summer adventures, one of which had been tag on this very float. The goal had been to force your target to leap into the water.

She dipped the soap in the water and went for Winnie.

"Not my hair!" Winnie screamed and ran toward the ramp. She got about halfway up before Katie pretended to give in.

"You are such a baby. I'll leave you alone, if I must. If you're lucky, maybe the mean seal will swim away when I jump in the water."

"He's back?" Winnie scanned the water. "Where . . . where is he? Maybe I don't need a bath after all."

"I'm sorry." Katie apologized, holding the soap behind her back. "I forgot how scared you were the other day. There's no seal out there. I was just teasing." By then she was nearly to Winnie, and when she was close enough to grab her, she wrapped a hand around her wrist and began smearing soap over her arm.

"Katie! That is so mean. Now I have to get back in the water." Winnie wiped at the soap, but it was hopeless. Her hand was dry, and none of it brushed away. Instead, she spread it around.

"That's right. Now, what happened to Sweetie?" Katie held the soap over her head, flouncing a bit as she walked toward the float. "I like it when you call me Sweetie."

"Sweetie's for good friends who don't smear soap all over my arm. You smeared. You're Katie from now on."

"Oh, Honey. I apologize. Forgive me?" Katie held out her arms for a hug.

"Okay. Just don't do it again." Winnie smiled, and she held out her arms in return to give Katie a hug. Just as they touched, Katie rubbed the soap vigorously up and down her back.

"Gotcha!" Katie hooted.

"No!" Winnie tried to pull away. "Stop! You apologized!"

"I was teasing! No! No!" By then they were off balance and far too close to the side of the float.

With arms flailing, and hands grabbing each other and empty air, Katie's foot missed the edge of the float first, and she stood off balance for several seconds as she realized what was about to happen. Winnie tried to disengage to save herself, but it was no good. Katie had a firm grip on her arm, and when she went completely off balance, the two women tumbled into the sea.

Neither one saw the splash, as they were underwater, but they both swam for the ladder as soon as they came up for air.

"It's cold," Katie grabbed at her towel. "I had no idea!"

"I told you. Listen next time." Winnie grabbed at the soap still in her friend's hand. "Give me that. I might as well get this over with."

When she got it, though, it didn't happen quite as Katie expected. Winnie was ready to give as good as she got, and she chased Katie across the float until Katie dove off the side to save herself.

"Chicken," Winnie called when Katie came up for air. "Here. You might as well use this. You can clean up your behavior, too, and be nicer to me." She tossed the soap into the water.

Katie swam for it with several strong strokes. It would sink if she didn't grab it fast, and it was the only bar she'd brought. She did take time to soap up before climbing out. She called out that on the second time in, the water was much more bearable, and she tried to sound very encouraging.

Winnie was having none of it, and she pouted, dipping her fingers into the water and brushing at her arm.

As she climbed out, Katie tossed Winnie the soap.

Either she would or she wouldn't. For now, she planned to dry and catch some sun. In Maine, that was the only way to warm after a swim.

It was the splash as she lay with her eyes closed that told her Winnie had followed through. Good, she mused. You can sleep inside tonight.

It was a pleasant and satisfying thought.

The water her friend splashed over her before she climbed out was far less pleasant. However, rather than giving Winnie the satisfaction of complaining, she sat up and laughed. It was a vacation, after all, and she was here with her good friend. If they couldn't take a little teasing from each other, then what was the point of it all?

Heading back to the house was their first big bombshell of the day. Walking past the old basement, from beyond the broken gate, a voice hailed them.

"Katie! Winnie! Hi!"

"Janine?" Katie looked at Winnie and shrugged before calling back, "We didn't plan for anyone to be here so early. But come on in."

"I know, I know, and I apologize." She came through the gate, her hands up in apology. "Oh, you've been swimming. Am I interrupting?"

"We've been bathing." Katie laughed and held up the soap. "With no running water, we have to depend on the island to keep us functioning."

"I'm so sorry. I should have remembered your gramma making you do that. Old memories are good memories, right?" She leaned in to Winnie, smiling. "Makes the city look pretty good, right?"

"Janine! Don't encourage her. I barely got her in the water." Katie drew a finger across her throat with a grin.

"Sweetie, what's that?" Winnie touched Katie on the shoulder and pointed through the gate, to where two boys were throwing sticks at each other.

"Oh, I should have said. I brought help." Janine yelled out, "Boys! Boys, get over here, and I mean pronto. And I better not see any black eyes when you get here."

"Are they here for the cookout?" The very idea worried Katie. That was specifically not what Jeff had promised. Katie planned to give him a fistful if he'd fallen through on this.

"Don't you worry about that. I roped their daddy in for the evening. However, he's off island for the day, so they're mine till the last ferry. I'm just putting them to work to keep them out of trouble. Boys! I said now!"

Two tow-headed boys came running up, both small, and wearing jeans and sneakers. Both had on striped tees that looked like the boys weren't the first owners. One bumped into the other when they stopped, and the first one kicked his brother on the leg.

The next two Katie recognized from town. The bigger one, Kevie, she thought, had the smaller one, Konnar, by the neck. Literally by the neck. He had his arm around his head, and he was giving him what she thought was a noogie, with his knuckles scraping his brother's head right on top.

"Stop that." Janine pulled his arm away, grabbing

the smaller boy's face in her hand. "Are you okay, Konnar?" When he nodded, she pointed her finger sternly at Kevie and made a demanding face. When she turned back to Katie and Winnie, she brightened with a smile. "You've met my olders. The two younger ones are Karlton, but he likes to go by Karl, and Keithie."

The youngest boys waved. The older two continued to wrestle with their mother's back turned.

"What can we do for you?" Katie questioned Janine as she waved at the four boys.

"Take these home with you when you leave? No, I'm teasing." She laughed as if embarrassed she had said that, looking at her boys before shaking her head. "Thank you though for insisting I come tonight without them. I've needed a break, and this will be nice. Now, though, I have a job for them to do."

"Doing what?" That had Katie mystified. She'd done lobster bakes. There was nothing to it. Build a fire, let it die down, and throw in some lobsters wrapped in foil. Even easier? Boil a pot of water on the fire and toss the lobsters in. She didn't have a pot, but since Jeff had made the plans, she assumed he'd provide the pot. Or pots, as it may be.

"You'll see." The boys had turned restless, and two now wrestled on the ground. "We have stuff to unload. If I don't keep them busy, they'll do this all afternoon. Al has the truck, so I borrowed Roker's for the day. You'll know it by the roll bars." She shrugged, as if the roll bars embarrassed her. "You just go on about whatever you were doing. We'll be out of your way in no time."

She had turned and was already heading towards the gate as she finished, her words fading as she reached to pop one of the boys on the back of the head before chasing them into the parking area.

"Sweetie?" Winnie was wide-eyed. "We have company."

"I know. She did promise they weren't staying long." Katie laughed. "And she's a very good friend from a very long time ago. Be patient, just for the day?"

"I suppose." She made a sad face, before letting it break into a wide smile. "For my very best friend? Absolutely!"

"Are you looking forward to tonight?" Katie wasn't sure she was, although it seemed it was happening one way or another.

Winnie made her viewpoint perfectly clear when she grabbed Katie's arms and squealed. "Lobster bake! I've never been to a lobster bake on a real beach. I'm so excited!"

Katie laughed. They were going to have a very good time. Winnie's reaction cinched it. Janine's boys? They'd be gone by then, and that was the icing on the cake . . . or maybe it was the butter on the lobster. Either way, if Winnie was this excited, it was going to be the best day of their trip.

17

"We can have cool air, if this window will just work." Katie wrestled with one beside the bed. It had raised several inches then stuck. She had her hand underneath it, shaking it in an attempt to force it up. The sun was now fully on the cabin, and with open rafters and no insulation, fresh air was paramount.

"I'm no good at windows, but I know we need some flowers in here." Winnie picked up her sunglasses from the desk. She had on pale blue shorts and a bright pink sleeveless top. The colors matched the beads on her sandals exactly. "Want to go looking with me?"

"Later. I'm working on this window." Katie was also in shorts, tan, with a teal-trimmed pocket tee. She wore her sturdy island walking shoes. She was down to inspecting the tracks on each side of the window frame to see what was blocking the movement of the glass panel. "In any case, we have to find a vase to put them in."

"Done. One water bottle emptied and ready." Winnie stepped out the door, and it banged shut after her. The sound of water splashed the deck.

"You could have left the water in. Something to cut them?" Katie yelled after her. "Most of the flowers up here have thorns."

Frustrated, she rapped the recalcitrant window pane with her knuckles, and got on the bed to open one of the two just above it. She bumped the wooden frame on the new window with her palm to get it started, and it slipped up with ease the rest of the way. "Why can't you learn this lesson?" she muttered at the partially opened window next to it. She could see Winnie already out in the woods, water bottle in hand, searching through the underbrush.

"The big purple ones are pretty," Katie called through the screen. "They're called lupines, but the best ones grow in full sun."

"I found some little white ones. There are so many I can't choose." Sure enough, there were several already waving from the mouth of the bottle. Winnie held it out with a smile for Katie to see.

"There's one place you have to see while you're here." Katie called through the screen again. "When you get all your flowers collected, we can drive there if you want."

"I'm ready now." She tucked something in her pocket and headed toward the cabin.

Once inside, Winnie set her collection of flowers on the desk, and she pulled her nail file from her pocket. "I love this." She held it up to show Katie then laid it beside the flowers.

"You love a nail file?" Katie reached to pick it up, and she held it in the light. "What in the world for?"

"It does everything. Like just now, I used it to saw off the flowers. Don't leave home without it. Do I need to change before we leave?" Winnie ran the comments together, fluffing her hair at the same time by running her fingers through it, and at one point, pulling out one of her blue combs and adjusting its position. She looked into a large hand mirror as she did so.

"We're going on a hike, so only if you're worried about stickers."

"We've hiked already this morning." Winnie let the mirror fall to the bed. "All the way to swim and back again. Besides, you said we could drive." She smiled prettily, as if pleading for leniency.

"We drive there. We hike up."

"A lighthouse? It must be a lighthouse. I've never been up a lighthouse." Winnie brightened.

"A mountain, although, before you panic, it's not a real mountain." Katie had to smile at the expression on her friend's face. "It's called Lookout Ledge, and it's got the best views anywhere around."

"Okay." Winnie sounded like it was somewhat less than okay. "No chairlifts, I suppose." She flipped the mirror over, toying with the handle a minute, before lifting it up and primping her hair again. "Still, if we can see everywhere, then everyone can see me. I can't complain about that. I'm ready." She dropped the mirror on the bed and walked to the door.

On the way to the car, just as they got to the gate, they found the few things Janine and her boys had unloaded amounted to a truckload, and not a small truckload at that. There were numerous folding tables leaning against the good gatepost, three galvanized metal tubs, and an enormous stack of metal folding chairs with slightly rusted joints. Four large and covered plastic bins apparently held *something,* but what they didn't know.

"Oh, my!" Katie was taken aback. "How many people are planning to be here?"

"Oh, it's like a real party!" Winnie grabbed Katie's arm and squealed. "Thank you, Sweetie! I'll climb any mountain you want me to, because I get to go to a party tonight!"

"Sure. Just for you." Katie smiled and patted her friend's hand in congratulations. The feelings running through her were a little different.

So, she thought. She was getting her wish. Jeff was bringing lots of people to talk to. Well, she had wished it, so she shouldn't be disappointed. She guessed somewhere in the back of her mind she had hoped for a little bit of her childhood back for this one evening. Oh, she knew in any case it wouldn't be more than a tantalizing tidbit of a time that had evaporated with the smoke rising from the remains of all that had been taken from her, but it might have been fun, anyway.

With her memories in tow, climbing Lookout Ledge was bittersweet. It was a designated town park, but parking was a grassy spot under the trees. To get to the ledge was a climb up a root- and moss-encrusted series of steps, with thick branches for handholds. The reward was a bare granite outcropping falling off into Carver Cove and offering unrestricted views across Rockhaven Island, showcasing the island's three massive wind turbines, and several large homes that topped spruce-covered ridges in the distance. They turned to take in East Haven Island behind them, and undulating hills visible on the mainland in the misty distance. All of it was held together by the deep blue of an ocean that reflected a brilliant and sunny sky.

Winnie oohed and aahed, and with her phone in her hand, she clicked and posted all that she saw. She posed herself with Katie, sending several selfies to the Internet kingdoms in the sky, and seemed enraptured with her mastery of this mountain throne.

Katie saw more. She pictured Babes at twelve, the summer before her final one, already buxom in her exuberant leap for adulthood, bundled up in a purple hoodie, with Apple at her side, trying to create a successful s'more over an open flame. They weren't supposed to build fires on the top of Lookout Ledge, but as kids, well, rules were made to be broken, and they had broken a few.

The sky had been heavy that day, with the wind filled with pending rain. It had spit at them occasionally, but it had yet to really open up on them, and being kids, they would only give in when forced to retreat.

Austie and Jeff had stood at the tip of the Ledge, flapping their arms and crowing like Jack in *Titanic*.

King of the World, they'd called. We're King of the World.

They had been, too. Katie guessed Benny and Bobby must have been there. They were with the gang constantly all summer long, so she couldn't imagine them anywhere else, but she couldn't picture them that day. Ritchey and Janine had been off island participating in some long-forgotten summer school function. No, that day had been just Babes and Apple, and the Kings of the World.

Austie. Katie remembered him as tall, in spite of not being much older than the rest of the gang. College tall, a real man, in body, if not in behavior. At least not that day. He had crowed, after all. Jeff, still fourteen, and looking very much fourteen. A head shorter than Austie, he could have been his midget twin, thumbs under his armpits, his face pointed to the sky.

They had called her over to join in their brash declarations of godhood to the entire world, but the edge of the ledge had warned her away, and she remembered being very cold. She'd escaped her grandmother's house with a jacket but left it on the gate as she ran down the road with her companions-in-mischief-and-mayhem leading her away.

Astray, she now thought might be the better word. They had done things she would be embarrassed to admit. The fire on Lookout Ledge hadn't been the worst. Oh, nothing too terribly serious. They'd been kids, but they'd explored what wasn't theirs to explore, houses with drives roped off for the earliest months of the year, boats moored and unused for the entire summer, and the occasional hidden beach, where they could laugh and be silly, and no one besides them would ever know.

It was Babes' last full summer on the island. In retrospect, Katie should have seen it as a warning, as the handwriting on the wall. *Watch out, Katie. I'm taking it all away. You've enjoyed this too much, and I don't like you having this much fun.*

So, there on Lookout Ledge with Winnie on a bright, sunny afternoon, there were two events taking place. One was two adult friends, snapping perfect, beautiful pictures and sharing laughter with each other; and a second, of a faded childhood that had been perfection, and those living it out hadn't even known what they'd had.

It wouldn't have mattered, anyway. When God decided to take it away, it evaporated completely. What was, what is, and what might be are three very different things. You can't hold to one, you have to live out the other, and the final one? That's a dark mystery that no one can plan out or depend on, and sometimes it never shows up at all.

That was Katie's day on Lookout Ledge, and she soaked up both memories, because they were both hers to claim.

18

Katie awoke from her nap to the sounds of screaming boys and large stones being tossed from the beach into the changing tide. She sat up to see her friend still asleep on the foldaway bed at her side. Outside the three younger Peavey boys ran rampant on her beach.

"No," she said. "They cannot be here."

The oldest, she thought. Kevie. Where was he? She'd seen them in action, and not being able to find one was disconcerting. She stood and slipped her shoes on, exiting quietly and hoping to let Winnie sleep.

At the edge of the deck, she snapped her fingers and called, "Boys!" They stopped and looked at her. "Where's your brother? Kevie, right?"

They all shrugged, but Konnar, the second in size,

said, "We dunno. He took off." They stood and looked at her, like they were waiting on something.

"You're Konnar, right?" She smiled, but she didn't feel a smile inside. Them not knowing? That was ominous.

"Yes, ma'am." He nodded, as if he was used to being just one of the bunch, and he rarely got his name used by outsiders.

"Thank you, Konnar. You may play now." She looked down the beach, and it took a minute before she noticed what wasn't there. When she did, it leaped out at her. "Konnar, where's the dinghy?"

He was picking up rocks a quarter his size and lobbing them to make them splash, and he paused just long enough to huff out, "Kevie," before he let loose his next volley.

"Oh, my word," she said. She scanned the water, hoping to see him on Dyer's Rock or at the lighthouse. There was no plastic dinghy. She took off down the shore path, knowing she would catch glimpses of the water all the way around the Point. If he had headed for the Cove—and where else would he have gone—she would find him at some point.

She pictured the lighthouse. The sun had been shining on the west side, and it was fully lighted. She figured in her head. It must be after five. Jeff had said he was coming early, and he hadn't been specific, but with the ferry times, five had stuck in her head.

Where was Jeff?

At every opportunity, she ducked past the greenery to see if the small boat was visible. With the tide high, the massive rocks dropped off sharply into the ocean, and she had no idea what she would do if she saw the boy, but at least she'd know where he was.

She was nearly to the path down to the dock when she got her first sighting, and it wasn't what she expected. Jeff appeared first, coming up from the dock, and then the boy appeared, his collar firmly grasped in Jeff's hand. Jeff didn't look pleased, either.

"Katie! I hoped to see you. Kevie here and I have been having a discussion, and I need you to clarify a point or two."

"She did, too!" The boy tried to wrench free from Jeff's hand, but he was eleven, and Jeff had a lobsterman's big hands and strong arms.

"I did what?" The boy's claim caught her off guard. She'd waved at him earlier when Janine had been there . . . and then she knew. This boy had been telling Jeff she and Winnie were bathing off the dock. How embarrassing! It had been perfectly innocent, but had the boy been spying? With what she'd seen, she thought it entirely probable.

"Hold that thought." Jeff held up one hand to her, his palm out. "Now that you're here, I want to ask Kevie my question again. Kevie, did Katie give you permission to take the dinghy?"

"Yes!" the boy spat.

"I—I—Jeff!" The boy was lying!

"Just a minute, Katie." Jeff leaned over and got right in the boy's face. "Kevie, she's right there, and whatever you tell me, she's going to hear. Make sure you tell me what really happened. Now, again, did

Katie give you her permission to take the boat out?"

"Well, she didn't say no!" His words still stung with their arrogance.

"Jeff! I was—"

He held his hand out to her yet again, interrupting her rebuttal. Instead, he asked Kevie another question. "Did you ask her?"

"How could I? She was asleep in there with her pink friend."

Katie was flabbergasted. She'd seen the younger boy kick his mother, but how could anyone be so big-headed? She had no idea kids could be so awful. It pleased her to see Jeff grab him by his ear as he stood.

"You little weasel. You know I don't put up with that nonsense. I should tie you to a tree until I take you home tonight. You don't deserve any lobster."

The boy barked back, "I don't want any lobster."

"Then I'd better not see you eating any, and I counted them. I know how many I brought." Jeff released him, and the boy took off over the top of the hill. He turned to Katie. "I'm sorry. There's nothing I could do. I had to bring them."

"All four of them?" She had spoken with Janine, who said her husband was keeping them. "Why the change of plans?"

"Al is why I was off island today. His truck had to go to Bangor, and I was supposed to be bringing him back. There was a fender-bender on the way, and he's having a broken arm repaired. Janine's on the ferry now to go pick him up." He laughed and shrugged. "Island life."

"But, you said you were taking that boy home to-night."

"Maybe. That one thinks I am, anyway. If Al gets out of surgery—"

"Surgery? My word, how bad was it?" The boy's antics with the boat seemed to pale in comparison to this. If it required a hospital stay, how long would that be? Poor Janine.

"You know fender benders. His arm was inside the steering wheel when he got hit, and it snapped it clean. Right through his shirtsleeve. The doc said he could probably be released tonight but driving would be out of the question for a week at least." He laughed.

"It's not funny. You can't laugh just because Al's not here." She didn't know Al, but laughing at him seemed insensitive.

"No. It's what he said in the doctor's office. Doc, he said, I can't drive, anyway. My truck's wrecked. I can still pilot my boat, though? I got lobster traps to haul." He laughed again, shaking his head. "That Al. They had him on something by then, so I suppose he can be excused."

"How will they get back, if he does get out?" She knew what last ferry meant. It meant last ferry, and that meant they were stuck on the mainland no matter what.

"I'll run over. I can take Janine for her car in the morning. Not a problem, as long as I go early." He made a motion with his hand, as if to brush it all off as old news. "Are you ready for a real lobster bake, one to shout out summer to the entire island?"

"I suppose?" She said it like a question, because she wasn't sure. "I saw all those tables. I don't know that I have room—"

"Come, now. There's lots of room."

"My deck won't hold all that stuff Janine and her boys unloaded. Just those tables alone . . ."

"Ah! Come here." He held out a hand, and when she offered hers, he pulled her to him and pointed down the path to the dock. Along the beach, the glistening stones shimmered in the afternoon sun. Roker from town and another man were unfolding the tables from up by the old gate. "We'll position the tables, and as soon as the tide moves completely out of the way, we'll set up the bonfire. More tables are already set up in the boathouse. You'll see later. Right now, how's Winnie doing?"

She pulled her hand free. Just for a moment, she'd let herself be lulled into thinking that fifteen-year-old boys matured into respectable men, and she really ought to give Jeff a chance. He had handled that boy masterfully, and to spend the day on the mainland to help a friend, only to have to go further and do more, including babysitting his children and taking his boat to the mainland to get him? Twice? That would be very expensive.

She remembered he had taken Winnie's hand the night before. His words rang out in her memory. *See you tomorrow. It'll be fun.* He told Katie he hoped she'd have fun. He'd known Winnie would have fun, or at least that he would have fun if Winnie was around.

"Why so many tables?" Her question was a distraction. What she wanted to ask was more along the line of, Why are you here? Why am I here? Why haven't you found a wife yet, Jeff Ragsdale?

Then, maybe the real questions should be aimed at God, as in, Why are you putting me through this again? Wasn't once bad enough?

Jeff was explaining with enthusiasm, though, all the people she would meet, and how they were excited to finally meet her. He didn't seem to notice she'd pulled her hand away when he mentioned Winnie's name. And why, of all things, would anyone on this island be excited to meet her? It had been half a lifetime, she had just been a summer girl, and the Point had sat abandoned and forgotten forever. Who knew and who cared? Not Katie, not God, and certainly not Jeff Ragsdale, who was more interested in Winnie Catron's happiness than he was about hers.

Just when she had been willing to at least give all this a try, and now God had to step in and bungle it one more time. Or, Katie was perfectly willing to admit, maybe it was like before. God wasn't stepping in, and that was the problem. He wasn't stepping in, and that's why things were falling apart, just like they had all those years ago.

19

The first few people arrived through the rickety gate, and somehow, that's how Katie expected everyone to come to the party. About six, the first boat showed up. It was a dinghy about the size of her plastic one, and there was a middle-aged couple in it. They looked like summer people, him in a paisley summer sweater and boaters, and her wearing a light jacket and chinos. They laughed when they shared that they had seen the bath on the float. They were glad their new neighbors across the Cove were taking advantage of the warm summer sun.

More came by motorboat, most small, but several lobster boats and one cabin cruiser tied up at moorings in the cove. Jeff set up a teenager with a small motorized skiff to ferry them to shore.

After a time, the float looked like the one in town,

the small boats stacked three and four deep, the latest arrivals walking over those already docked to get to the float.

Ashore, adults corralled children, and teens explored among the trees. Someone had put bright yellow tape around the old foundation, with signs that said off limits. It seemed to be keeping most people out, although Katie knew that as far as the teens wandering the point went, they would see it as a challenge hiding something too good not to explore.

Jeff even had an athletic-looking teen girl giving the younger children rides in the plastic dinghy out and around the Lil' Dude. A stack of orange life preservers was in one of the plastic bins delivered by Janine that morning.

At the crescent-shaped beach by the dock, Roker and the friend from earlier had a driftwood fire roaring, with a large bucket of banded lobsters to the side. They would go on as soon as they had coerced a good bed of coals from the flames.

Jeff seemed to be the center of it all. He directed, he pointed, he requested, and things moved just the way he intended. The children knew him, and he knelt and played with the younger ones; the older crowd he called out to, and they called back. The adults seemed to think him a friend, as if there was a very real connection between him and each one of them.

Most surprising to Katie was the number of people who spoke to her. They were very polite, introducing themselves as living on this cove, or on that harbor, or on the road that led to yet another part of the island. A surprising number mentioned that they hoped to see her in services the next morning.

The fire had been knocked down, and the lobsters were being prepared, when Katie caught what Jeff was doing. As he greeted people, he shook their hands, or sometimes gave the women a formal kiss on the cheek. Then, invariably, he searched until he found her, and pointed them her way.

She wanted to roll her eyes at that. She didn't appreciate being the poor summer waif whose home and chance for a lifetime of enjoyment on Rockhaven had been stolen away by a freak late-season fire. Let it go, Jeff, she thought. This was all your idea, and I gave in only because you forced me into it. I don't want to be singled out. I don't want people to feel pity for me.

For a distraction, she searched for Winnie. She had been angry at her earlier, yet she hadn't been at Jeff's side at all. She hadn't seen her anywhere, and that worried her. Winnie liked to be at the center of everything. The young woman was a dear, and Katie adored her, but her natural beauty had shaped who she was. She was so used to being admired that she expected to be admired. Ignore her, and she didn't understand why the world was behaving as it was.

Prowling, carrying a glass of clear soda in her hand, Katie finally found where her friend had gotten herself to. As she neared the cabin, she caught the sound of giggles and high-pitched laughter. Once she stepped on the deck, she saw the culprit. Inside, Winnie perched on Katie's bed, and she was surrounded by probably a dozen preteen and teen girls. Spread out before her were all her makeup supplies, haircare ointments, and other pretties for making herself beautiful. At the desk, an island girl with medium length hair was trying—not very successfully—to work Winnie's curlers into her hair.

"Winnie?" Katie knocked and opened the screen. "Are you having fun?"

"Oh, Sweetie, more than I ever thought possible! Your Jeffie said I would, and I am. I really am." Several of the girls giggled when Winnie called him Jeffie. She didn't seem to notice, though. She reached to point to a girl who was putting eyeshadow on with one of Winnie's application pads. "Oh, right there. You missed a tiny spot."

Katie laughed. "Enjoy, Winnie. I'm going to mingle." She turned away and stepped outside, not sure if her friend had even heard her. She had been wrong about Jeff and Winnie. She had to have been. They didn't seem to have spoken more than a dozen words to each other the entire evening, if that. Her good friend Winnie was still her good friend Winnie, and she was glad.

It dawned on her that she hadn't seen Janine's boys creating havoc the entire evening. She frowned, wondering how bad the damage would be if those boys had found a way to escape observation for any length of time.

"Katie, there you are." Jeff stepped on the deck, and he walked up to her with a smile. "I see Winnie's doing what she really enjoys. I know you especially like her, but I can't imagine spending my life with someone who likes makeup better than the outdoors. I'd rather dig in the mud any day."

"I remember you digging in the mud." Katie smiled.

"Seriously? After all this time, I thought you would have forgotten anything like that." He seemed very pleased with her remark, and he rocked up on the balls of his feet with a smile.

"It's on your Facebook page, remember?"

"Oh. Right. You and Winnie are friends, and she probably showed you. I didn't think. Man, you scrolled a long way down if you found that picture."

"That was a long time ago, wasn't it? I also noticed it was faded around the edges. Torn in one spot, too." It felt good to talk to him. Not to worry about what she said. Not to have to explain herself. Just to say what came to her.

"It was my mirror you." He bumped her arm with his elbow. "You were there smiling at me when I got up in the morning and when I went to bed at night."

"You didn't know I was alive." She teased, but it was true. She had been the summer friend who slipped in and slipped out. The others had been the true twine, all wrapped into a ball, one, and complete. Except Babes. She unraveled first, then Katie, then she supposed Ritchey was the final straw. She hadn't heard anything about the other four.

"Oh, I knew. I just didn't know how to talk to you."

"Hokey-smokey. That's nonsense. You talked to me all the time. Can we borrow your boat, Katie, or you knock down the hornet's nest first, Katie. You talked all the time." She laughed. She had forgotten much of that until now. Being here with Jeff, with the people milling around, offered a kind of security. She could relax, because it was safe to let her guard down.

"We did used to say that, didn't we? Hokey-smokey. I'd forgotten. Yeah, I said that stuff, but only because I didn't know how to say anything else. I talked to you like a boy because I didn't know how to talk to a girl." He took a sip of his soda, and without warning, he pointed. "There's one."

"One what?" She looked for a hawk, or a deer.

"A Peavey. I have them all assigned to church members, one per boy."

"Like wardens." Katie laughed, then she looked away, embarrassed. "Oh, I'm so sorry. Don't ever let Janine know I said that. I had wondered why they weren't running rampant over the landscape. You, you have a fix for everything, don't you?"

"I hope." He looked at her and smiled, raising his eyebrows and letting them fall down again. "Have I fixed everything?"

"I don't know. What needed fixed?" It seemed to her that he had fixed a lot of stuff already. Her dock, the cabin, the Lil' Dude. "The gate. The gate's not fixed. One post is rotten through."

He laughed. "Not exactly what I meant, but I can do that, too. If I do, will you promise to come back to enjoy it?"

Katie knew what that meant. Come back and enjoy him was what he meant. She didn't answer. She didn't know how to answer.

"Okay. I'm pushing too hard. So, have you enjoyed my church?"

"Your church?" It hit her. Not just some, but almost everyone had invited her to church the next day. She'd not thought too much of it. She and Winnie had planned on going all along. Now it made sense. "These people are all from your church?"

"Mostly. A few attend sporadically, but we are kinda a one-church town. If someone attends, yeah, they're from my church." He motioned to where one of the smaller Peaveys tugged against an older woman's grip on his arm. "That's why I take so much interest in Janine's kids. Not because they're wonderful, because they're not, not to spend time with, anyway." He chuckled. "Don't you tell Janine I said *that*. Still, those boys are part of my church, and I've always felt responsible for them. It's why I step in when Janine and Al need a hand."

Katie felt her eyes burn, and she chewed her lip. Why was he saying this to her? No man could be this generous with his time and emotions. This evening, all clearly planned by Jeff. The Point, all clearly maintained by Jeff. Janine's rough and tangle family, all clearly kept functioning by Jeff. When did Jeff do *Jeff?*

She was angry, too. Look at these people. They clearly enjoyed each other. They were well-mannered and polite, but they were here, and they were having a good time. This was what she'd wanted all those years ago, why she had looked forward to returning each summer. This was what God had stolen from her.

For her the knife thrust even deeper. This man standing next to her. What could have grown between them if they'd had a lifetime to get to know one another? What could their lives have become?

"Katie? Is everything okay?" The words were soft and caring.

Katie knew them for what they were, though. They were the same soft and caring words he had offered to Janine and all these people around her on her beloved Point: You need a hand. Can I step in?

That was not what she needed from him. Her emotions were on quicksand, and she was about to go under. She did the only thing she could think to do.

"Peachy. Hokey-smokey." She waved her hand in the air between them, wriggling her fingers, and she laughed. It was to keep from looking at him. "You throw a fine shindig, Jeffie. I think it's time to head to the bonfire and see if those lobsters are all fired up." She turned away from him and headed up the hill. She continued to wave her hand over her shoulder, waggling her fingers as she went.

She heard him call behind her, "Jeffie?" but she didn't dare slow down. She was afraid the tears would fall if she did.

Katie traced the rafters in the dark.

Well, the almost-dark. A sliver of a moon was out, and it cast just enough light that she could make out almost everything in the small cabin. With no shades, and windows running completely down each wall, a lot of light came in.

She had done her best to avoid Jeff the rest of the evening. He had cornered her once or twice, and she had adroitly skidded the conversation onto safe ground, bringing up old times to laugh about, or telling him funny stories from Winnie's modeling gigs. The last hour she'd been surprised not to find him at all. She'd looked, but he was nowhere. She'd seen Roker at the fire, tamping out the final bed of coals, and getting ready to spread them out on the stones to let them die. The incoming tide would do the rest, and in the morning there would be nothing left. She asked about Jeff, and he was surprised she didn't know. He'd left early to get to his boat. He had received Janine's call that they were on the way to meet him.

The rest of the evening had been on her shoulders. After Jeff's remarks about Janine and her boys, she went out of her way to say farewell to them, one at a time, from the smallest to the largest. The order had been intentional; as she was afraid she would lose her nerve if she approached the oldest first. If he kicked her, she would run in terror from the others.

Poor Winnie. She'd learned a new lesson today. Beautiful can't be given away. It's a gift to some people, and those who don't have it sometimes want it so badly it devastates them. The girl with the curlers had expected her hair to turn into Winnie's brilliant halo of perfection. Instead, she'd still sprouted a poor haircut, split ends, and drooping curls. She'd cried at the end, and Winnie hadn't known how to console someone in a situation she had no familiarity with.

She imagined Jeff on his boat, alone, gunning his engine just because he could, with the spray from the biggest swells flinging itself over the boat. His broad shoulders and his flyaway hair would be the silhouette Janine and her husband would see from a distance, and they would know their friend had come to ferry them home.

Did they know what they had, how special Jeff was? Who did that sort of thing for other people, just because they needed him?

She looked at the moon out the window. The day

had been warmer than most, and the window was open several inches. The smell of the sea mingled with spruce and crushed clover swept in on the sounds of a tide that even now, in the peace of the night, brushed silken fingers along the rocky shoreline. All those years ago, she wondered, did I realize what I had, how special Jeff was? He said he hoped he'd changed. What had he meant by that? What was she missing out on? What had he been trying to fix, if not the Point and the damage of fourteen years; if not the Lil' Dude, the boat on which she'd learned to sail?

Come back to enjoy it. He'd said that to her, and it had sounded like an invitation. Of course she'd be back. This was her home, even if her grandmother's house was long gone. Rockhaven wasn't gone. Carver Point wasn't gone.

The next one she whispered out loud. "Jeff's not gone."

Ritchey was. He was gone to Texas. Babes? She'd been gone longer than Katie. The rest, except Janine? Not a word, except Austie, maybe piloting airliners across the friendly skies.

Jeff was here. She was back. That picture on Winnie's phone, Katie and Jeff in their mud-streaked youth, and smiling just because they were there, in that place, and at that time. In that picture, to those people, they hadn't looked to the past and asked it whether they had permission to be happy, and the future hadn't been on their radar. That moment was all they had, and they had grabbed at it, and they had been happy. That picture said so.

Why was this so hard for her? Forget the past. Brush aside the future. Grab today.

She wanted to, but that burned-out hole still loomed, she had to be in Boston next week, and she still had a car payment to make. How could she toss all that away for the memory of a boy she'd once known?

She turned in her bed, trying to find sleep. The mattress control on the little table at her side lighted up, and something clicked. The generator outside hummed, and she felt the mattress adjust itself underneath her. It reminded her of Jeff. Everything reminded her of Jeff. Even the sound of the generator humming her to sleep in the dark.

Somehow, she was aware of the world fading around her, and then the rafters turned dark, and she was gone.

21

Sunday morning shrouded the little cabin in a blanket of fog, and the misty swirl of sea air muted the sounds of the island. It was a morning for coming to life slowly, and life under the weathered, shingled roof whispered.

"Did we survive the lobster bake?" Did they survive over a hundred people and more food than should be served at any one time was what she meant. Katie rolled over and pushed at the lump on the smaller bed. "Are you alive under there?"

"Spa!" A hand appeared from underneath the electric blanket. "Spa! Warm bath! Please, Katie!"

"Oh, you!" She pushed the hand back under the blanket and pulled her own bedding to her chin, seeing the window still open next to her. "It's chilly this morning."

"It's chilly every morning. Next summer, I want an inside potty. Mark that on your list."

"Sure." Katie smiled at that. She might as well go it all. "And a jetted tub. How would that be, with marble counters and heated floors?"

"Seriously?" Winnie's face appeared from underneath her blanket. "You would really do that?"

"Honey, my family once had money, but it's been gone a long time. I'm lucky to have this."

"And your potty." She disappeared once again.

"That, too, and I think it's time." Katie threw back the covers and pulled on her robe. She might as well be warm.

By the time she returned, the first rays of sun were trying to beat away the fog, and the sea could just be seen beyond the deck. The trees dripped with the silky touch of a summer Maine sky that had come to brush early morning earth.

"Honey, sun's coming out." Katie shook Winnie's shoulder. "Church in a couple hours. Time to climb out of bed."

"Oh, I do have to go." Winnie threw back the covers and stretched. "My turn."

Once she was out the door, she called to Katie, and she began to sing, "Rock-a-bye baby . . ." One hand knocked on a window.

"Are you okay, Winnie?" Katie looked out at her. "What is it?"

She pointed to the water, starting up again, "Rock-a-bye baby—oh, Katie! Come save me! Quick!"

"What, Honey?" When Katie stepped outside she

laughed. There was the seal, just out of the water, warming in one of the few sunny spots on the beach.

"Shush! Be quiet as a mouse, Katie. It might attack us. Sing with me. Rock-a-bye . . . oh, I can't remember the words!" Winnie shook her hands in frustration.

"Watch." Katie leaned off the deck and picked up a big stone. She tossed it close to the seal to where it would make a lot of noise. She took a surprised step backward when the big creature turned its head their way and barked at them.

"Katie! Be careful. Stay right there while I go inside. I'll call 9-1-1 for you." Winnie sidled sideways, while starting up again, more softly, "Rocky-bye-baby, don't come this way . . ."

"Stop it, Winnie. It's scared of us, too. Just wait a minute." At least she thought it was. It hadn't run, though, and she knelt for another rock. She picked a bigger one this time and tossed it just beside the seal. This time, at the clattering sound, it rolled, twisted, and slipped into the water.

"Oh, girl, I was so scared! I really have to go now." Winnie tapped Katie on the shoulder to move her aside, and with her arms in front of her for balance, she gingerly danced down the path to the outhouse.

"What next?" Katie hit her forehead with the palm of her hand. She stepped back inside just as the sun broke out, fully lighting the edge of the deck, and sending shards of light lancing into the room. "Oh, how beautiful!" She turned to the window and looked out to the water, the Lil' Dude just visible in the wisps of fog still encircling everything out at sea. It was gone at the cabin, though, and it seemed she was in a magical fairyland, like something absolutely wonderful was about to happen. A change in her life, perhaps. Whatever, she knew it would be just what she needed.

A ferry horn sounded, and Katie realized the fog had thrown her timing off. They had slept through the sunrise, and that meant they were going to be in a rush.

"Is it still gone?" It was Winnie calling from the far edge of the clearing. "Can I come across?"

"Come on. You're safe if you run. Hurry!" Katie opened the screen for her friend.

"Why? Will it chase me?" Winnie ran through the door, her hands in the air like a criminal surrendering after a holdup.

"No, it's not that. It's something more important than any old seal. The fog messes up the time, and now it's later than I thought. We have to prep for church as fast as we can." She threw her big case on the bed and flipped it open. Her church best was inside. It wasn't actually very dressy, but it also wasn't shorts and a tee. A pressed denim skirt and summer shirt would have to do. It was just right for her island walking shoes.

Winnie was at her side, and she had a difference of opinion. "No, no, Sweetie. I cannot let you torture everyone in that cute little church we drove by. We have to get you something better to wear." Winnie began to drag one of her cases over.

"Honey, we never drove by the church." They'd seen the steeple, but that was all. Katie was pretty sure of that.

160

"You're right. That was Jeffie and me that went by the church. Now, let's choose you something pretty." She situated her case next to Katie's and snapped it open. She pulled out a blue silk dress with a burgundy thread woven through it and held it up to her friend.

"This is too much." Katie laughed, shaking her head. "Even if it fits, I didn't bring shoes to go with this."

"But I did." From underneath the dress, Winnie pulled out a pair of blue sandals with burgundy beads that just matched the threads in the dress. "See? Just like mine."

"If they fit." Katie held them to her feet. "I don't know."

"You think they fit me? Of course not. See this strap?" She pulled at a thin strap across the heel. "I can get three sizes out of this. A freebie from a Neiman's call."

"They are pretty together. I'll give it a try." If Winnie wore something equally flashy, Katie was pretty sure they would be the most overdressed pair at church. Still, it was sweet of Winnie to offer, and she did appreciate it.

"We'll knock their socks off. Now, let's see about your hair . . ."

Katie decided to give in and go with it. It seemed she would be beautiful this morning whether she liked it or not.

22

Arriving at the church was the first surprise.

"Look, Winnie. It must be a special service today." It did look that way. The church sign out front was low to the ground, and it had a large, hand-lettered sign wrapped around it. In block letters it spelled out WELCOME BACK.

"How sweet! Reunion Sunday." Winnie pulled out her phone. "Let me see . . . um, Rockhaven Town Church. They do have a website! Give me a second, yes, it is a special Sunday. Oh!" She looked up.

"What?" The lot in front of the church was very full, except for one spot next to the door. Katie pulled in. "Nice. The best spot."

"It may be somebody else's. It says Reserved." Winnie held out her phone. "Maybe we should come back another time. We might be intruding."

"Intruding? It's church." She took the phone, though, and she read the website banner for that morning. CELEBRATION SUNDAY – DON'T SPILL THE BEANS! "So it's the pastor's anniversary or something. It'll be fun."

"What if this is his parking space?"

"Or hers. The pastor could be a woman, you know. By this time, if she's not here, she's not coming." Katy undid her belt and let it retract. "Look, Jeff's car." Sure enough, just around the corner sat the green Jeep with the black fabric roof.

"Think he saved us a seat?"

"Let's go see." She would be surprised if there were any seats to save. She'd attended here numerous times growing up, and it wasn't that large. With all the cars, she expected it to be standing room only, and they weren't late.

Before they reached the door, the first couple from the evening before greeted them, this time in coordinating summer suits. Katie felt more an honored guest than a one-time visitor, but it was nice. She attributed it to the party the night before, and it had been a party. Perhaps the enthusiastic greeting was gratitude for allowing the church to use her property.

In the foyer, she was surprised to find the Peavey Four neatly dressed in suits and ties. The eldest, Kevie, handed her a red rose, and he bowed his head and said, "For you, Miss Katie." The other three echoed, "Welcome, Miss Katie."

"How cute!" Winnie held up her camera and snapped a picture of them. "You boys are adorable."

"No, we're not." Konnar growled those words, barely getting them out before Kevie elbowed him on the shoulder.

"Not so cute," Katie whispered to her friend. "I've spent time with them."

The second surprise of the morning was the huge banner across the front of the church.

WELCOME BACK KATIE CARVER TO ROCKHAVEN ISLAND

"Look." Winnie pointed.

"I can see. I'm not blind." Katie was startled to have Roker take her arm and lead her to the front of the church. Arms reached out to them as they walked by, people saying hello. She recognized most of them. Janine was one, and a man stood beside her with a cast on one arm. She waved and smiled. Two empty seats were waiting, and Roker deposited them on the first row.

So, Katie decided. All this must have to do with last night. Why would it be a secret, though? She hadn't talked to anyone. Who was there who could spill the beans to her? She hadn't known anyone before last night. She laughed, hiding it behind her hand to keep it quiet.

"What's funny?"

"This. I'm trying to decipher if we're the guests of honor, but we can't be. We parked in the honoree's parking place, though. Of that I'm pretty sure."

"That's you up there. I can read, you know." Winnie's eyes were on the banner.

"Small churches do this. They save seats for

164

guests, and the sign? I did host them out at the Point. Believe it or not, even I know that's pretty special out here. People don't just show up on private land for lobster bakes."

They had been whispering, and the organ started up, drowning out their conversation. They stood as the ministerial staff walked in from a side door. Their third surprise? Jeffrey Ragsdale wore the ecumenical vestments of an ordained minister. He caught her eye and smiled at her, giving her a nod.

A lay leader came forward first, asking the congregation to stand, and together they sang a familiar song, calling the faithful to Christ. Afterward they were asked to bow in prayer as special thanks were offered for fourteen years of prayer that was being answered on this glorious celebration day.

Katie frowned as she glanced at Winnie, but her friend had her eyes closed. This couldn't be what she thought it was. Still, fourteen was a number that was too coincidental for her comfort, and there was all the rest: Jeff sending his "parishioners" one by one to greet her yesterday out on the Point; the parking space she now suspected had indeed been reserved for her; and the signs that weren't just for the average visitor. Dear God, she breathed. You had better not let this be what I think it is.

The first few lines of the prayer told the truth of the matter, though. The words thanked God for keeping watch over their good friend Katie and allowing her to spend time with them once again; for protecting her from the dangers of the world, and allowing the devastation of the past to be wiped clean.

The words reached deeply into Katie, and they awakened old pain that was worse than anything she had felt in years: her grandmother, her parents, her friends that had been lost forever. How could he use the words *keeping watch, protecting,* and *wiped clean* about her life? God had done no such thing. No. He had left her in her hour of need, and He had not been there for her since.

She would burst if she listened any longer, and in a moment of desperation, she slipped past Winnie. She tried to walk, but she was running by the time she reached the door. She broke into the sunlight and felt the tears burn in her eyes.

Ooh, she thought, clenching her fists. If only she'd stayed in Boston, gone to the Bahamas, maybe. Anywhere but here.

"Katie?"

She turned to see Jeff walking toward her. She laughed, sensing it sounded a bit manic, but feeling the frustration she fought welling up and not knowing how to disguise it any longer.

"I don't understand. What does that mean?"

"Why didn't you tell me about this?" She pointed to the sign, then to the church. She fought to keep the tears inside. "How could you expect me to have that thrown at me and not be offended?"

"How could I stop what I didn't know about? I realize this caught you off guard. It caught me off guard, but they did it because they are wonderful, caring people."

"But you told them. How else would they know about me?" That ripped at her inside. All these years, and she had told no one about Jeff. He had been her pain, and she had let no one know. She felt violated.

"How could they know? Because I told them? Yes. I did that. That's wrong? If so, yes, I was wrong. Since you left that final summer, I've waited for you to come back. You were all I talked about to anyone who would listen. Katie Carver this and Katie Carver that. Everything we ever did, they know. I've loved you since we were kids." He looked away at that, and he took a deep breath. "I'm sorry. I shouldn't have said that. But I won't take it back."

"What about my privacy? How could you do that without me knowing, without asking me if it was okay to tell my life to people I don't know?" She'd heard his words, though, the ones she'd wanted to hear all those years ago. Could it ever be enough, after all she'd endured? She'd hurt so much!

"You may not know them, but trust me, they know you. And Katie, how could I keep it quiet?" He took her hands in his. "I spent the entire summer I was sixteen on the Point. My dad and I put the float out, and I walked the drive with a shovel, filling in the low spots. I hoped you'd come that year, maybe with your parents, and you never did. My dad said to give you a year, let you turn sixteen. You'd be able to drive then. Keep the cabin up, and one day you'd be back. Every year I thought it would be the year. Then I went away to college, and when I returned, I didn't think you'd remember me any longer. I hardly remembered me.

167

That first summer back, I went to the Point, and it was a wreck. I knew then that if you ever showed up again, I'd make sure it was ready for you when you did."

"Why?" The tears really did flow this time.

"Just in case, Katie. You might come back, and I did it just in case."

"That's not what I mean. Why didn't you come find me for all those years?"

"I tried. I tried so many times. I called. I left messages. Your dad, and your mom, too, told me I was just an island boy, and I had no place in your life."

"No. They wouldn't. Not Mom and Dad." It made sense, though. Their refusal to return, cutting her off completely from the island. She suspected they would have sold the Point if her grandmother's will hadn't left it to her, something she'd learned only in the past year.

"I want to show you this." Jeff reached into his vestments and pulled out a worn, stained envelope. It was stamped and sealed, and across the address had been printed *Rejected. Return to sender.* "I was eighteen when I sent you this. It was the first time I was brave enough to tell you I loved you. I invited you back to the island to live here forever. This is why I went away to school. I couldn't bear to be here where I was reminded of you every day."

"You came back, though. Why the change?" Her emotions were a pendulum. She wanted this, to believe in all of this. She really did.

"I did. I came back. I went away because I couldn't bear to live in this place that reminded me of you everywhere I went, but I came back because I had to be in this place where I was reminded of you every single day. I had to have as much of you as I could get, even if it was only memories."

"And if the Point had been sold? My parents wanted to."

"The island has tax records. They list the owner. Your name automatically went on the deed when you turned eighteen."

"A transfer-on-death deed from my grandmother. I only learned that last year. I had to be eighteen to gain control, and my parents chose to never tell me. Even then, it still could have been sold. All your work would have been wasted."

"As long as you were on the deed, I had hope to hold to. If hope was all I ever had, I couldn't let go of you." His eyes were red, and they pleaded with her. "If I had said nothing about you, these people still would have known. Everything I did out at the Point was out of love for you."

Katie looked away, trembling with the emotion that overtook her. All this time she'd tried to lock her memories of Jeff away, and all this time, he'd been soaking up every one. How could she have skewed so far away from the one thing that had ever been really important in her life? She wiped at her eyes, trying to blink them clean.

"Katie? Was I wrong? You did love me. I know you must." He was silent for a time before he stepped forward to look in her face. "Do I have permission to still hope?"

"You know, I blamed God. I could never forgive Him for everything I lost. You. For losing you." She looked into his eyes, understanding now that love worked in more than one way. All those years that she had pushed the memories of Rockhaven away, Jeff had been here preparing Rockhaven for her return. "I know better now. God brought me back to you."

Jeff smiled. "I knew that from the moment Marc called and said you were coming back to the island. I never doubted God for a single minute."

She wiped her face, finally understanding her estrangement truly hadn't been God's fault. All those years, and He had kept her chances alive, in spite of her. He hadn't stolen them from her at all.

When Jeff wrapped his arms around her, this time she didn't push him away.

From the church, cheers and clapping broke the quiet of the island morning.

Katie looked up at Jeff. "Do they always know everything that goes on around here?"

"When it comes to you, yes. I couldn't hide the way I feel about you if I wanted to, and trust me, Katie, I don't want to."

It was a hand on Jeff's shoulder that broke up the intimate moment. Roker said, "Son, you've got a lifetime for this. The rest of us in there? We want lunch, and we want it on time."

Katie enjoyed the service, more than any she had ever attended before. When the final prayers were said, she had something of her own to say, even if no one else heard.

"God, you didn't take my life from me. You kept it for me until I was ready to return. I can never thank you enough for that."

"And for your good friend, Winnie. Thank Him for that, too." Winnie put her arm across Katie's shoulders, whispering her words softly.

"And for Winnie, even if she does snore at night." Katie smiled.

"Eh! I do not." Winnie was smiling, though.

Katie looked up at Jeff, so proud and fine in front of the entire town, and she was convinced of one thing. Her Rockhaven summer was turning out to be the best one she'd ever had.

www.ingramcontent.com/pod-product-compliance
Lightning Source LLC
Chambersburg PA
CBHW070935250626
47159CB00009B/3253